THE PROVIDENT FAMILY

of

BAXTER'S YARD

A NOVEL BY

CORNELL CHARLES

Published by Afterwords Press, Hackensack, NJ

First published by Afterwords Press, 2012

Printed in the United States
ISBN 978-0-9854327-0-6

PROLOGUE

There were many anomalies unique to the island of Au Tabor because of some dozen changes in military occupation that followed eighteenth century periodic battles and conquests between the two major powers of Britain and France.

After Britain won the final battle, English was affirmed as the official language and the territory was under the sovereign rule of the British monarchy. However the spoken but unwritten French patois dialect was more widely used for communication by a large African population. They suffered severely as a disadvantaged people with feelings of inadequacy and from a lack of skills needed to cope with language impairment. As a consequence, the majority population of Au Tabor was largely illiterate following colonization by Britain.

An Anglicized government with adjunct constitution was imposed atop a culture and religious education that was unmistakably Gallic. The result was a British-French mishmash of governance and education, ill defined and confusing to the psyche of the island's people. The inscrutable truth was that in spite of the overwhelming French Catholic orientation of the population of Au Tabor, the local body of scholars, prominent political figures, teachers and artists emanated mainly from the non-Catholic community.

A cultural dichotomy of sorts existed with the French giving their blessing to a mix of local festivities harboring mysteries and fables, while the British endeavored to stamp out vestiges of other inculcated traditions by an insistence on showing loyalty to the preeminence and rule of the British throne.

The attention and worth bestowed on the population of African origin did not rise above those of a workhorse status. Selected authority failed to treat them above the level of a commodity with only their service being requested and was evident in the prosperity and diversity of the newly arrived citizens in relation to those who have been around for generations. The parks for recreation of citizens and memorialized places of interest of peace and advancement were erected in honor and at the behest of an earlier electorate who prided themselves with goals of a finer civility. It is fair to note these traditions were aimed at posterity; however succeeding communities throughout the years hankered after the privileges, supremacy and wealth but not the commonality and decency for a pastoral and idyllic existence.

THE PROVIDENT FAMILY

of

BAXTER'S YARD

A NOVEL BY CORNELL CHARLES

1

Victor Provident was considered an exceptional student in primary school. His behavior was exemplary, a factor his teachers thought noteworthy considering that he lived in an environment not known for producing boys with such outstanding qualities. Although fourteen years old and a few years above the average age of other applicants, he was in the first group of boys selected to be interviewed to attend St. Teresa's College. The college was established by priests of a French religious order, Fils de Marie Immaculée, on Au Tabor Island at the commencement of the twentieth century. The island is part of an archipelago and is anchored in the Caribbean Sea.

A foreigner in a white seamless gown reaching to his ankles made Victor unsure about the stranger's gender. His father had instructed him only about attending an interview for admission to college, but was not given further details. The stranger's deep bass voice filled the hall with authority, startling Victor.

"Calling Victor Provident!"

It was Herman Provident, Victor's father, who rushed forward first in obvious anxiety. Victor had never seen his father so nervous and compliant, virtually shouting and nodding his head jerkily in affirmation.

"Yes, Father. I will, Father. Not yet, Father. Soon, Father. I thank you, Father Giraud."

During the interview Victor remained silent while his father responded to the questions Father Giraud had read off a paper and which his father had answered diligently.

Victor turned to his father as they stepped out the door after registration. "Where are his children?" Victor assumed someone addressed as Father would have children.

"Victor, he does not have children. He is not allowed to have any."

"Why you calling him father and he's not your daddy?"

"Because he is the father of our souls and the other kind of fathers look after bodies."

As they walked home, Herman waved and tipped his hat to persons walking by with the notion they knew he had successfully registered Victor as a student at the college. Meanwhile, Victor squinted against the sun's glare and in his pre-pubescent mind thought quietly about the differences in dress between men and women. The unusual item of clothing which he thought only women wore and the unexpected bass tone voice of Father Giraud seemed unnatural to him. Before leaving, Victor was cautioned by Father Giraud,, "It is the kindness and generosity of good souls who saw your need and promise. I hope you live up to their expectations."

Victor recalled similar snippets of Christian teaching told to him by the wife of retired Col. Simpson for whom he did odd jobs. He believed people of her kind knew a lot more about how to be good and behave properly compared to the folks in Baxter's Yard. He had heard that one of their great, great grandparents knew someone who had come down from the heavens, and the good things he taught them were passed on.

2

Soon after Christian missionaries arrived on the island of Au Tabor and built churches and schools to facilitate the imparting of religious education, they took on administrative roles and taught the island natives new lifestyles, other world histories and fascinating events.

The predominant segment of the population was of African heritage. They were vague on details of when their predecessors first set foot on the island. Occasionally, an uncomfortable whisper or a rebellious drunk would acknowledge a heritage of slavery, however the riddle of who brought them to the island, when and how they arrived was unknown. Most people did not want to know, as they believed it conferred on them an inferior status.

The children of Au Tabor first learned that entry into the world was by means of a large white bird called a 'stork' flying with an infant in a hammock attached to its long beak and delivering him or her to their parents. Parents allowed this representative version of childbirth, perhaps fearing biological explanations might encourage sexually explicit thoughts and unseemly questions, or to shirk the humiliation of a blank and untraceable heritage.

And so an adaptation of their primal history was eagerly fitted into midstream of other civilizations. Captive minds relented in servility to a call for a new modesty with superfluous clothing. Dogmatic laws imposed through spiritual education erased primal narratives and were replaced with stern canons from another hemisphere, magical and unfamiliar as a wintry season.

3

Between many fashionable buildings fronting the streets of Tabor City, were earthen alleyways leading to backyard spaces teeming with shanties. This haphazard collection of shanties seemed to be jostling each other for space. Elegant homes all had street frontage and low-income tenants rented house lots in the yard behind them.

Herman and Victor paused before Miss Mable and Nurse Grace chatting out of opposite windows at the entrance to the yard. The glow of a proud father was evident in his profuse salutations.

"A very good morning to you Miss Mable, and the same to you Nurse Grace. My son makes me feel proud today," Herman said, beaming to the occupants of street-front homes at the alley entrance. "He is now a student of St. Teresa's College."

"Congrats, Victor. Well done," offered Nurse Grace. "You should be proud of him every day, Herman. I always know him as a good boy."

"Now don't let down your father and mother," Miss Mable, the landlady and eldest of the spinster sisters, chimed in. "You must study hard, don't follow bad company and always set a good example. Forget those vagabonds who are always making trouble and cursing. I know you will make a man of yourself."

Herman nudged his son in the back. "Say thanks."

"Thank you. I will try," Victor said quietly.

Victor's mother, Lorna, had told residents of the Yard about Victor going to the secondary school. It was a source of pride that spoke of a child's academic ability and the family able to afford the fees.

Miss Mable Baxter was the largest renter of house spots in the yard behind her residence known throughout Tabor City as Baxter's Yard. She monitored the tenants' sundry activities and social life, often acting as arbiter of frequent disputes. Herman Provident was an able and willing handyman, and he was being rewarded for exemplary conduct with a Mable and Diana Baxter scholarship to his son Victor. The community in the Yard was supposed to note this gesture, both as an incentive for good behavior and to quell the impressions of Miss Mable as an indiscriminate miserly spinster.

Herman quickened his steps into the Yard when Bajan Tilley in the house just behind Miss Mable's fence alerted him about a dispute concerning Lorna.

"That no-good Iris causing trouble again with your lady."

Herman hurried through the crowd that had gathered and excitedly encircled the adversaries Miss Iris and Lorna. A surprised Miss Iris promptly adopted a protective stance on seeing Herman.

"I am somebody dat always try and avoid trouble. I don't mind people business. I have no time for dat, so don't interfere with me," cried Iris looking around anxiously for an opening to make an exit.

The crowd had inflated around the three participants, shutting all exits and they yelled provocative statements into the arena hoping to enliven the contest.

"You lie! Is your habit to make trouble and interfere in people business and say bad things about them!" a woman yelled from among the crowd.

"So why you saying the man have something with Miss Mable?" a male voice shouted.

"Who me, you hear me Iris say dat?" Iris said as she slapped her flat chest and looked in the direction of the voice.

Herman walked menacingly up to Iris. Her tense shoulders and chest visibly heaved beneath her clothes and the crowd yelled out to Herman, "Burse her tail!" "Give her some licks!" "Don't spare her!"

Herman was a mild-mannered individual not likely to prolong the altercation or to be spoiling for a fight. Instead he waved his forefinger inches from her face and warned, "Next time you open your dirty mouth, make sure it is not about me or else I will get the same Miss Mable, who you bad mouthing, to throw your backside out of the Yard."

This threat had maximum impact on Iris, a resident of Baxter's Yard for twenty plus years. Aware of the tolerance granted Iris in the refuge of the Yard despite frequent disputes, Herman was sure this action would be effective.

As the disappointed onlookers dispersed along shoulder width tracks separating the hovelled dwellings, young males tossed out unflattering remarks. "Why he not doing nothing? What she say must be true."

"But look like he really controlling Miss Mable."

"Yeah yeah, imagine he goin make the bitch throw Iris out."

Herman, with his arm around his wife Lorna, confidently steered her into their hut ignoring snide remarks from women who had returned to squat before enamel basins of clothes soaking in sudsy water.

"Why she think she better than us, eh? Lord, tell me," asked Agnes the youngest of the women as Mr. and Mrs. Provident disappeared into their home.

"And she only there with 'My husband dis and my husband dat.' I could of have many husbands too if I wanted," boasted Granny Katie.

"But nobody would want a coo-yon like Herman for a husband," doubted Agnes.

"Is a competition going on with Miss Iris for who Ma Baxter like best," added Granny Katie.

"And for who get scholarship and who don't want pay rent," Ma Reggie declared with a signature laugh of ridicule.

"Ha ha hye, woooeee."

4

"Ay, ay, what he looking for, something happen to bring police in the Yard?" A squatting Ma Reggie stood up abruptly to sound an alarm as soapsuds dripped off her hands into the basin of laundry at her feet.

"Anybody do anything why police looking for somebody?" she continued.

The policeman looked an incongruous figure, his wide brimmed cork helmet and white tunic just about filled the space between two dingy huts on either side of the alleyway. He moved forward gingerly, picking out dry ground with each footstep to avoid soiling his polished black boots till he reached an open section. As he looked around, his eyes met with hostile stares and vulgar gestures from residents.

"Messier, so people car even quarrel among themselves, they have to send for police?" complained Agnes turning and thrusting her bottom out in the direction of the policeman.

"I here long enough to know she does send Bajan Tilley out on the street to look for policeman and is Tilley self who tell Ma Baxter," Granny Katie concluded.

"You know I did see when she did pass dere. I never trust her. She's a real suceur that Tilley," Ma Reggie spoke angrily. "I ready to beat her if she ever cross me."

Confrontation and harassment by constabulary personnel pervaded Baxter's Yard. The residents appeared frequently in court and were a sizeable number of the prison population. As a group ensnared within a lower economic and social status, they did not submit easily to local state laws citing the dearth of community facilities and services within the Yard. In reality, official personnel were aware that the compound residents often illicitly helped themselves to services provided by utility and other essential service suppliers. Some residents who migrated from the countryside regularly returned to amass food supplies from the farms of relatives.

Many disturbances within the Yard stemmed from a lack of privacy. All amenities were exposed and detached from the main hut in full view of neighbors. Two steps away was a shed assigned as a kitchen. The shower stall and water faucets were to one side with the latrine hut furthest away, giving it standalone prominence. The huts were built square-shaped with full-length cedar planks from nearby forests were precariously supported at each corner by three to five random sized boulders placed on top each other. The earthen ground beneath the hut was shared by fowls seated on hatching eggs and crabs with periscopic eyes emerging stealthily from underground. The roofs and exterior boards were covered with overlapping moldy shingles in a pattern similar to fish scales. Family unit allotments in the Yard were marked out by the foot worn tracks meandering between the huts.

This part of Tabor City was a green, wooded area during an earlier period. The trees filtered the sun's blistering light, held firm against buffeting storm winds and turned violent rain showers into tame flowing streams.

It was now a trampled soil without a sign of life, only a dead tree stump remained as a favored stool of an amputee, his crutch resting at his feet among lifeless root tentacles.

As early evening approached, a cloud of aromas assailed nasal passages with an indivisible bouquet of cooking blends replaced later at twilight by the distinctive savor of roasting coffee beans and, occasionally, roasting corn.

Coal pot fires were extinguished in a rite of sundown marking a day's end to food preparation as bedraggled youngsters drifted home around the twilight hour. The sounds of chatter in the Yard increased, and as night fell, the huts appeared to huddle closer together with the clamor of voices from inside, some filled with profanity. The pale yellow light of candles and kerosene lamps glowing unsteadily inside the huts were now being cloaked in darkness as shutters closed securely and newly discovered gaps in the partitions were blocked with wads of paper and cloth.

Peculiar calm seeped into the nighttime around the midnight hour when a silent space was given to frail elderly ladies for an appalling task at a minimal wage. At the furtive hour they carried a putrid matter in tall pails, euphemistically referred to as 'night soil' for disposal at a dumping site.

5

axter's Yard's southern entrance adjoined Anse Zordi, a beaching base for boats belonging to area fishermen. The land behind it was steep and pockmarked with shanty structures that appeared to be tumbling on top each other.

Bay Street ended at the waterfront on reaching the shore of Anse Zordi. The sea current swept into the bay, transporting all the floating trash tossed into the water some distance away. The litter collected among fishing implements and canoes resting on the shores of Anse Zordi.

Across the street was a row of two storey houses, past residences once owned by middle class workers, now transformed into bars, drinking holes, pleasure houses, and small grocery shops with minimal inventories of canned corned beef and sardines, flour, sugar and rice, cooking oil, laundry soap, candles, matches and cigarettes.

Many adults flocked here just before sundown to purchase supplies of fish as the canoes streamed in with the day's catch. There was a self-imposed after dark prohibition for all youth and many adults since to be seen then in the area suggested a lifestyle of suspect depravity.

Victor and his teenage friends never joined the crowd at the frequent squabbles in Baxter's Yard. After registration at his new school, Victor hastened home to change his clothes and then ran to the bay of Anse Zordi.

Most of the canoes had sailed out at daybreak for a day's fishing, and the vacant spaces provided Victor's friends, Colom, Planche and Blackie, an opportunity to search among the litter for anything of interest. Colom, the eldest, alerted the rest. "Look, Vicious reach."

"You went up by where dem priest living?" announced Planche.

"Yes, I am going to the new school them starting."

"So that mean you going become a priest I suppose," guessed Planche.

"Me? Never! Me put on all that cloth those priest wearing?"

"Is the same amount ladies using for a dress?" Blackie sought a linkage.

"Boy, a lot more, the cloth reaching from neck to foot and so much cloth covering their arms that it flapping like seagull wings."

"So you think if they stretch their arms and legs wide so, they can fly like seagull." Planche extended his limbs to illustrate.

"You see that fella, Planche? If you just tell him one thing, he goin to think ten extra thing on top of it," warned Colom.

"Planche, boy, they came here by boat, they did not fly," teased Victor.

"Anyway, it have enough cloth to make sail for canoe?" Blackie asked, still curious about the clothing.

"C'mon Blackie, you forget it taking six flour bag sew together to make canoe sail." Colom usually chided the others by stating known facts, a strategy that often resulted in no further comment.

"Look, Chalky coming," Planche noticed. "What's that he have in his hand?"

"A dry coconut," Victor noted, "and he makin style as usual."

Chalky knew they would be all over him, cajoling and begging for a piece of coconut.

"Break the thing nah," urged Colom impatiently.

"Alright take it easy." Chalky appealed for calm.

"I know Chalky will always gimme so I not begging," said Blackie as they encircled Chalky who stood his ground watching them drool.

"Well, give the man room to....look, look a big rock, break it on that," Victor directed.

Chalky complied and thrust the dry coconut against the rock. The coconut splintered and everyone scrambled for a piece except a surprised Chalky whose face turned angry and then tearful, perhaps because he was denied the right, as owner, of dividing the coconut among his friends. He refused to be consoled by an offer of a piece from Victor and instead left hurriedly shouting in a threatening tone, "I going to tell my daddy! I going tell him you all steal my coconut!"

Chalky's father was a 300-plus pound hulk called Ballast. As a fisherman, he earned this name because a canoe in which he sat had to strictly limit the number and weight of equipment on board. He was reputed to have won a fight against three men and for this reason was feared in the community. As expected the young boys fled to selected hiding places.

6

Au Tabor was partitioned into three political constituencies, North, Central and South. A rolling census attempted to maintain each constituency at a level of one third of the total population of 90,000 ensuring electoral boundaries followed a demography defined by number limits irrespective of acreage size or terrain.

An important contribution to the island's economy was found in sugar cultivation in the fertile valleys of northern Au Tabor. The valleys had the appearance of a vast green carpet of willowy grass sprouting out of slender calibrated stems, an eye-catching scene when viewed from the surrounding hilltops. A bonded human species with backs curved beetle-like among the tall grass defoliated lush acres and were first detected by the glint of sunlight on cutlass blades. The severed stems were assembled and transported to factories where they were fed through grinding teeth of steel rollers to extract every ounce of sugary liquid from their capillaries. The liquid was then centrifuged until it became sugar crystals. Some of the sugary liquid was developed to a thick syrup stage called molasses, which was fermented and distilled into various grades of refined alcohol and rum spirits.

Cane sugar, a sweetener in demand provided the owners and agents of supply a status of wealthy sugar barons. The field workers subsisted in a settlement of huts covered with bundles of dry sisal grass and floors of earthen compaction. At sundown, the active supervision in the field ended and the colony of illiterate workers was left to satisfy natural impulses, which invariably supplied new members for the workforce. Some frustrated males assembled in next-door drinking holes where unrefined alcohol was served as a mood changer that either suppressed or emboldened seething desires.

The constituency also had the largest acreage with its agriculturally oriented population of estate owners and bucolic farmhands. They were easily recognized in their pragmatic wear of khaki twill outfits during visits to the towns and places of commerce.

South Au Tabor was a tourist Mecca of manicured landscapes and a glitzy uniformity of hotel room units of precise size and structural design. Liveried attendants with hedge clippers threatened the advancing leaf and twig like gatekeepers on the lookout for resurgent contenders. A flurry of attendants trained in the arrangement of bed linen and cutlery placement could be seen scurrying between numbered rooms, kitchens and dining tables endeavoring to make life unique, exotic and comfortable for their foreign guests. Irate guests arrived with problems they hoped would be calmed in waters lapping sandy beaches or would melt away under the warmth of sunny days. Many also arrived for romantic beginnings or to heal soured relationships in the aphrodisiacal environment of a tropical holiday.

Some guests of imperious manner demanded their money's worth by displaying extreme intolerance and were likely to cause disturbance in the tranquil atmosphere. Workers trained in emotional restraint were predisposed to accept responsibility for any claim by a guest of a deficiency in service.

Before the land of South Tabor was scoured for the tourism plant, coastline estates were cultivated with orderly rows of coconut trees that aligned the gleaming curvature of white sandy beaches. The tumbling thud of dried brown nuts was among few uneven noises at variance with the constant prattle of coconut palms waggling in light breezes and the muffled hiss of surf scurrying at intervals along the seashore.

The native islander was sympathetically made to feel his life in reality was tedious and static in an enclosed field of night and day, weather of sunshine and rain, and distant horizons, highlighted at sunrise and sunset. Tales of a wondrous life wrapped in layers of fantasy stirred a craving for a better life in the reverie of another country.

With a nature of extraordinary conviviality and openness the islander was helpful in welcoming the various persons visiting their paradisiacal island. Many of the visitors expressed an overwhelming desire to purchase land on which islanders had become habituated.

Payment in a currency of fluctuating value and an opportunity of an alternate lifestyle prodded the habituated islander to hand over his affixed wealth to an established coterie of investors. The land was frequently employed as a tax hideaway. If developed as a resort, access was usually restricted and was invariably partitioned outside the social framework. This could result in an uncomfortable social adjustment for the next generation as usually island tourism investment mobilizes to attract mainly the wealthiest patrons.

Administering and linking the North and South constituencies was Central Au Tabor, home of the capital, Tabor City. Perfectly aligned city streets running north to south were intersected by those running in an east to west direction, apportioning the city into a checkerboard of square lots popularly referred to as city blocks. A public park with war monuments, water fountains and very old trees occupied some notable blocks. The block across the street from the recreation park had an aura of perpetuity with an imposing structure of a hundred year old church of Victorian architecture with an equally impressive designation "Cathedral Basilica of the Immaculate Conception."

Government administrative offices, the Halls of Justice and Parliament were other important structures filling square spaces. The rest were filled with mainly gable-roofed, eighteenth-century, colonial-style wooden houses squeezed next to each other. With few exceptions, houses rising above one storey had covered balconies protruding from second floors over pedestrian sidewalks parallel to city streets. The ground floors of the majority of those buildings were used for commercial purposes of various retail trading, professional offices, and small craft facilities such as tailoring and shoe repair service shops.

7

Lorna made regular stops to chat with her friend Bajan Tilley after her weekly grocery shopping and always included a token gift. Today it was a flask of locally brewed rum.

"Thank you, my dear, for seeing after my rheumatism. These nights have a chill in them. How is the family? Sit, sit," insisted Miss Tilley, pointing to a wooden stool next to her cushioned rocking chair beneath the window. As long as the window was open or the jalousie louvers lowered, rest assured the chair was occupied. All articles in the tiny room were tidily put away giving one the notion every item sat untouched in their places.

Lorna had a vested interest for keeping Miss Tilley in active communication because of her vantage location as the first house behind Miss Mable's fence and all traffic into the Yard had to go by her window.

"Everyone fine by the grace of God, I have to be thankful to Him for my son."

"Miss Iris not interfering with you after the last time?"

"Not since my husband put her in her place. But why she after me like that, I have done the lady nothing," Lorna said and waited for an explanation.

"Well, she is a lady who does be jealous of people a lot. Open your eyes for how she does be jealous of the attention Miss Mable give you husband and now the scholarship. Me, I don't want to add to your worries."

"You don't think that woman is a witch?" Lorna asked, hoping to encourage Bajan Tilley to disclose more of what she knew.

"Two nights ago she pass here with a young boy going out after midnight. What a woman like her could be doing outside after midnight," said Bajan Tilley on cue and provided more reason why Lorna should be concerned.

An increasingly alarmed Lorna had some advice. "Ehh! And you ain't telling Miss Mable what you see."

"Me, for Miss Mable to tell the lady I told her so and so, and next thing you know it's on me the lady goin work all her evil tricks."

"My husband is sure the few things she has on a tray selling cannot pay her rent and feed her. He thinks this is to fool people while she carrying on with her black magic."

"Even Victor from the time he was a little boy tell me how Iris is a funny lady and he did not like her because she always chase him and his friends if they playing by her house."

"Once a boy was trying to catch a crab underneath her house and she threw a basin of water that almost wet him and he told somebody it is because he heard voices coming from inside the house." Miss Tilley liked to sneak hearsay into the drama and Lorna was right on cue.

"But this is not the first time I hear people talk about strange noise and voices coming from her house especially at nighttime. I don't think anybody ever see inside her house. It always lockup tight, tight."

"Even though you look inside, you will not see anything because the spirit thing only moves around if it is very, very dark."

"One day I would really like to see what that spirit she has looking like, but I won't want it to come near me."

"Very few persons have ever see a real spirit unless you in that business yourself. Otherwise they make sure to keep it out of their home."

"And so how they keep it out?" Lorna asked, genuinely concerned.

"You have to spread some garlic in front your door."

"Garlic, you said?"

"Yes, garlic or spices with a strong smell," Miss Tilley said, nodding her head. "Crush it under your shoe so it would look like an accident if you do not want your husband to know. They say the smell does burn it eyes and make it blind and you can hear like it wings beating as it escape."

"Like it reach in Miss Mable house already. Maybe you should tell her what to do!" Lorna and Miss Tilley rocked and swayed in laughter.

"So it look like the spirit we are talking about, when it take charge it does make a lot of things happen to people. The worse thing they ever do is suck blood from people, especially children, so don't take no chance," warned Miss Tilley.

"They showed in a cinema picture something like that, it look like the bats flying around here at night, but this one live overseas."

"Could be a cousin, who knows. Some things belong to Satan and the devil."

"Now you sound like my Herman. Dat is what he does call the man in Germany name Hitler who want war with the King in England."

"The best thing is to praise God for all mercies." Tilley reassured Lorna who looked increasingly nervous.

A subdued Lorna seemed to have heard enough. She sighed and

stood up and lifted her bag of groceries. "Me, I not taking any chances. Look, without even knowing I bought some garlic. Anyway, till another day, God willing. Bye for now."

8

The following night Herman arrived home wearing a worried look, "Lorna, look here!" he said seeking her attention, "Just now war will declare overseas, so prepare yourself for that."

"Eh eh, so how I must prepare myself?"

Herman did not anticipate the question. He had merely intended to transmit the news. "Do you know what it means if England and the all Commonwealth go to war?" Herman called attention to a wider involvement.

"So, with all that happening you will still want to send Victor to England to become a lawyer?"

Herman shrugged his shoulders and went into another room.

The confrontation between the European allies and Germany following the invasion of Poland by Germany in the winter of year 1939 soon escalated. It was official, a World War had been declared. English families on Au Tabor were frantically cabling relatives at home to find out if brothers, sons and nephews had been conscripted after learning all men between the ages of twenty and twenty-one had to register for compulsory military service.

Every evening in neighborhoods, groups of men gathered around the few wireless sets on the island and listened to news, relayed compliments of the British Broadcasting Corporation, of the progress of a war declared in Europe. Radio wireless sets encased in varnished wooden cabinets, owned by the wealthy were dutifully turned up to maximum volume for the audience standing on sidewalks outside listening through jalousie windows.

Allied military personnel arrived on the island in increasing numbers and could be seen in all parts of the island. Victor and companions befriended them as word of their generosity spread quickly. Confectionery and other snacks from the canteen attracted an entourage around military personnel.

On Au Tabor, impressions of war were transmitted by cinema newsreels showing weary soldiers in action on the battlefields along with the patriotic songs sung proudly on the island. Scarcity and rationing of essential goods were the main inconveniences experienced on the island. The days were bright, sunny and undisturbed by the conflict. The nights, however, seemed unfriendly and dismal as all one hundred and fifty motor vehicles on the island were ordered to paint a thick, black "T" on each headlamp to reduce the light beam, and households covered light bulbs to achieve an imprecise dimness so the island would hopefully not be discerned easily at nighttime. Residents watched the powerful searchlights beam among the stars in search of attackers from the sky and a sense of patriotism to the British Empire welled up in their bosoms.

A money shortage and scarcity of essential goods created an era of bartering across Au Tabor. Many services, medical, legal among others were exchanged for live fowls and ground provisions; local sweets and fruit were bartered for safety pins and clothes buttons; empty bottles and used postage stamps could earn a matinee ticket or some groceries.

There was hardly a disposable item. Containers, as well as contents, were equally preserved for multiple uses. Emptied wooden and cardboard boxes were main storage bins kept beneath wooden bunks, and newspaper was perhaps the most utilized packaging material after it was no longer being read. Potters shaped the good earth into household and cooking utensils and tinsmiths converted empty tins and cans into various kitchenware.

Households were creatively engaged in processing and were largely self-sufficient in essential supplies. Local vegetables, fruits and provisions were plentiful. Sundry items replacing imports such as the cream of boiled cow's milk whipped into butter, cooking and healing oils processed from coconuts, medicines were mainly herbal; hats, mats, brooms came from a variety of straw plants; mattresses filled with fiber from dry coconut husk, cushions and pillows stuffed with fowl feathers, sisal plants turned into rope and twine, calabash and bamboo utensils. Patched clothes and half-soled shoe bore no stigma.

The little garbage accumulated was a mutable mix of food remnants promptly acquired by pig owners and converted to pig food following an extended boiling process on an open wood fire.

The creativity of the youth played out in various sporting exercises. They enjoyed running in tandem with hand-propelled discarded bicycle rims, barrel hoops and worn tires.

Lightweight balsa wood provided young craftsmen material for toy boats and rafts and other sea related enjoyment.

They challenged wind currents with kites made from leaf spines of coconut palms and pitched marbles in a game called 'zing.' The young girls spent hours practicing skills for a game of 'tick-e-tock' that entails hand juggling with selected pebbles.

While adults felt tension from the vagaries of war and the enemy, the joys of an intrepid youth was seriously hindered by a local archenemy known to Victor and friends as the "wicked devil."

They feared a much older boy named Margay who did not seem to know anything of his own past. He referred vaguely to remembering someone telling him an aunt of his was living in the area, but so far he was unable to find her. He was first noticed delivering newspapers around Tabor City and slept in a recess beneath a flight of stairs at the back of the newspaper building. He took a delight in tormenting Victor and his friends and although they shunned him, he would invade their peaceful play activity with destructive intent. When Victor and friends were flying their kites, Margay warned he would attach a razorblade to the tail of his kite to cut the string of others while in the air. During a game of marbles, he asked to play with his solid metal ball bearing that would splinter their marbles on contact, and even as they spun their wooden tops, he claimed the spinning tip of his top was sharpened to split open others as it landed on them.

"They should send mate to fight war in Germany so the British could shoot his backside," suggested Victor who really hoped Margay would be sent to fight on the German side so the British would get him.

"You want to send the man to help the Germans? Boy just now they will call you a traitor," Blackie observed.

"They could still send him on the British side but put him right in front so he will get the first bullet from the Germans and the same time shelter those behind him," said Colom, always with the final declaration. Such was the desperation among the group to be rid of the nemesis in Margay.

News filtered from the battlefield of two Taborian lads listed among recent casualties of the war in Europe. The news was received with a mix of pride and sadness. Au Tabor claimed its heroes in the war and some saw this as a badge of honor for the bereaved families.

This stimulated citizens into patriotic fervor and to commemorate every strategic advantage gained in battle that was announced over the radio.

Still, many locals envisioned the war as a compilation of made-to-order excitement, of bravado among falling bombs and dodging bullets to emerge alive as a celebrated and medaled hero. These stereotypes were impersonations of propaganda news broadcasts of allied radio stations and cinema newsreels.

This romantic notion of war ended on a Tuesday night in March 1942. In the reputed safe harbor of Tabor City, the brightly lit passenger ship S.S. Lady Nelson belonging to the Canadian National Steamship Company was berthed alongside the wharf and unintentionally exposed the unlighted cargo ship the S.S. Umtata berthed ahead. Approaching midnight, Tabor City was suddenly awakened by two thunderous explosions. A German submarine delighted in the sitting targets, fired a torpedo into the stern of the Lady Nelson and minutes later followed by another torpedo into the stern of the Umtata.

Every household in Tabor City was jolted from sleep by loud explosions and had to quickly come to terms with waking to the reality of war munitions exploding in the neighborhood and dismiss any thoughts of a nightmarish dream. Before long, city streets were surreal scenes of residents in nightwear fleeing to the outskirts of Tabor City. Ahead of them, stevedores and shipping personnel were fleeing to regions furthest away from the docks. Many sought refuge with relatives or friends on the outskirts and others took protective cover on reaching the first cordon of dense bushes and trees outside the city limits. A terrified populace now envisioned World War II as truly global and had reached Au Tabor. Not knowing the location of the enemy or when and where next they would strike in the total darkness contributed to the horror of the night.

At first light, some details of the incident were circulated among the traumatized refugees in their various hiding places. Eventually it was deemed safe to return to the city and note firsthand the actual episode of the night and ensuing confusion. The evacuees returned to find everything was as they left — untouched and unmoved.

Both steamers sank in the relatively shallow draft of the harbor berth and were resting on the seabed with the main upper decks still above water. The Umtata manned by an East Indian crew and with empty cargo holds was awaiting an offer of freight.

The Lady Nelson, due to sail within a few hours of being torpedoed, was severely disabled and a total of thirty lives were lost between crew, passengers and dockworkers.

Humbled by the torpedo event, the people of Au Tabor developed a mix of respect and fear of the enemy as clever and deceptive, for while the allies were searching the skies, the enemy was attacking from beneath the sea.

However, no one would have imagined this tragic war incident would have turned a grim situation for a traumatized city's population into a bountiful occasion. Having lost all electricity generating power, the luxury passenger liner could no longer keep in store a specific quantity of food supplies requiring refrigeration. Wartime rationing and laws against hoarding of basic food supplies were temporarily abandoned on Au Tabor to allow for gouging of the plenty from the disabled liner. This posed yet another paradox because residents and shop owners did not have the required refrigerated storage capacity for the available quantity of bulk food items and desserts. So the bonanza lasted exactly two days with all classes of persons sharing, and after that period many food items had to be dumped because of spoilage.

To guard against future submarine attacks, Army and Naval engineers constructed mesh netting that stretched the full width across the narrow entrance to Tabor City harbor to protect ships berthed alongside the wharf from torpedoes. The net had to be maneuvered open and closed to allow the passage of large ships.

Winston Churchill became a household name, revered as worldly, wise, courageous and famous. He was revered as an iconic figure and many newborns were named after him.

Victory in Europe against the Nazi regime was anticipated and citizens were ecstatic over the two-day holiday in the month of June 1945 celebrating the victory known as V.E. Day. A memorable portrayal by a well-known local promoter of social and cultural events dramatically expressed local sentiment. A handcart with an effigy propped upright and labeled 'HITLER' could be flogged for two pennies with a whip from a tree branch. Victory over Japan followed soon after and the island welcomed another festive celebration. The promoter, ostentatious and garrulous after his earlier caper, entertained the community on this occasion with a flogging of an effigy of the alternate enemy, Japan, labeled 'TOJO.' It could be whipped for one penny.

9

While the war had ended officially, local minds deferred in transition. The disbanding of army personnel had family and social implications with most being absorbed into government institutions.

The youth of Tabor had viewed a career in the armed forces with ambition. The pride and honor of being eligible to strut around Au Tabor in military uniform lingered and transitioned among youth in schools as well-organized uniformed members of cadet corps, scouts, guides, cubs and brownies. These groups participated in every parade and paid homage to patrons of military orientation.

The first group of schoolboys admitted to St. Teresa's College returned to school in January at the start of their third year. Among them was a secular bond between four students delighting in each other's youthful vitality and talents. Victor Provident was the streetwise guru; Martin Innocent plotted the group's escapades, Thomas Blyth, an athlete and playboy, and Vivian Keswick, the academic whiz kid. Their mothers were fervent attendees of church services, a prudent policy while their sons were under the religious tutelage of the Roman Catholic clergy. Although there was disparity in their family social standings, the camaraderie of the four students was strong in the course of their budding adolescence.

The clique of four was renowned for their guile and tomfoolery. After many warnings, a stern reprimand with threats of suspension was being considered by the headmaster for a series of complaints received from persons in the community accusing the clique of name-calling.

Because parents and godparents submitted complex names with pride and hauteur at baptism, perhaps in resentment, a community responded with names suited to their dialectic affinity. The replacement aliases were usually chosen with peculiar ethos and often depicted a noticeable deformity. The intention was not always to offend, a paradox often received with mixed reactions. In street theatrics, a complainant protesting a given alias was repeatedly provoked by onlookers, especially if the reaction was belligerent.

Poor driving skills resulted in frequent accidents and earned the town's postmaster, Mr. Blanchet the nickname, "Mr. Reckless" conferred by students who provoked him with a display of excessive caution whenever his Ford car was approaching.

None of Mr. Blanchet's features conformed to a pleasant appearance; his eyelids lifted reluctantly and more often looked down his nose, which spanned the full width of his upper lip. His face had a look signaling a disagreeable personality helped by a voice that began as a growl and ended in a nasal whine.

Shouts of "Reckless, Reckless coming," rang out among students walking home on a suburban road at the end of a school day. The gang of four signaled the school crowd into a mock safety practice of exaggerated precaution by climbing onto road embankments and jumping into roadside drains as if avoiding oncoming danger. While this infuriated Mr. Blanchet sufficiently to lodge a complaint, the youngsters were amused by their construct of avoiding danger.

Those who could not accept the provocation by student pranksters reported them to schoolteachers, parents and police.

A report to the police was lodged by a city employee when teased and nicknamed "Mosquito Mothers' Man." His official job was to identify and eliminate breeding places of mosquitoes. Moreover, he was mosquito-like, puny, walked with shuffling steps and limbs bent at the joints, his deep sunken cheeks receded beneath a pair of bulging eyeballs, and because of his work and interest in finding breeding places, he was caricatured as the boyfriend of mosquitoes. On one occasion, Martin and Thomas saw him and his crew of workers cleaning a breeding place, the two youngsters pretended to be swatting mosquitoes on their arms and legs, and despite nonstop abuse, Martin looked at his watch and commented, "Its four o'clock, it should be time for the men to knock off."

"Don't come and time my men because when I does be wid your mudder and sister you doesn't time me," the Mosquito Man shot back amid peals of laughter from spectators pausing to view this short theatrical skit. There were no directors and producers, only actors with an impromptu and uncensored script.

In his admonition of the four students, the headmaster considered the harassment of Lizzie as the behavior most despicable. Lizzie had obvious mental and physical disabilities within her dwarfish, rotund body. She had the profile of an overstuffed doll with an abnormal looking Cyclops eye so peculiar and spellbinding as to obscure the presence of the other normal eye. Schoolchildren harassed her; idle passersby ridiculed her bloated body with taunts of 'Lizie the stuffed doll, Lizzie 'popot booway." She grumbled constantly in a monologue of gibberish to all and sundry.

Margay, the bully, constantly teased Lizzie. And as often as he teased Lizzie, she would chant a refrain. "You will soon die bad in hell."

When Margay died tragically after falling off a mango tree and sustaining a broken neck, the public stopped teasing her. They assumed her words were ominous and had prophetic results.

Following this incident, it was not easy to avoid Lizzie on the streets of Au Tabor. She seemed unhappy walking the streets unnoticed, missing usual social interchange and would intercept any and everyone with the same jingle, "You hear what happen to Margay, I had warn him, I had warn him."

10

The fourth form was the penultimate class and year before graduation and disciplining of students in that class was intensified by school administrators. The overall conduct and their adherence to the specified school uniform were more rigidly enforced. Any clothing, headgear or attire that bolstered impressions of manhood was banned even outside school hours. The wearing of long pants, felt hats and caps were not allowed. The St. Teresa's College uniform was a dressy all white shirt and short pants with blue blazer worn in tropical sunny weather along with a white cork helmet as the only headgear permitted.

Local parents were respectfully silent on the quirky rules, customs and mannerisms. Apart from uniforms unsuited to the local climate and culture were the added idiosyncrasies of some teachers insisting you "button your blazer or take it off."

Any foible of a student was not treated with sympathy and understanding but met with encouraged ridicule and made popular terms such as the "howler." A blunder in any activity, including sports, was mercilessly derided with taunts from the entire school body. A student reporting a disgraceful act by others to the authorities was met with scorn for the untrustworthy offense of "sneaking." There was the quick-witted French master from a neighboring island who asked a student to conjugate the French verb (tenir). The students accented pronunciation was not up to standard as he commenced "Je tins, tu tins, il tins," so the French Master interrupted with a ridiculing, "Yes, Nous bucket, Vous skillet, Ils tot. Now stand on the bench, Jackass."

Many parents just able to pay attendance fees fell far short of managing the uniform costs of helmet, blazer and all white uniform with attendant laundering costs. Certain privileges were used to honor and reward prefects, top sportsmen and committee heads by permitting them use of stairways and pathways prohibited to the general student body.

Methods used to regulate, conduct and apply punishment were adopted from public schools in the motherland of the robed and cloistered educators. Corporal punishment was transposed from rowdy home-style beatings with a leather belt to an orderly and precise whipping of seven strokes with a wooden cane. This took place in the office of the headmaster who tucked the oversized full-length sleeve of his robe up over his shoulder to permit a free swing of the arm when flagellating the bent-over student's buttocks. A standard function of the office was for administering punishment, which was assumed whenever a student was requested to proceed to the headmaster's office.

Friday afternoon assemblies marked the official end to a school week and always began with the awarding of Alpha and Beta honors routinely earned by a small clique of high achievers. Then the names of students failing academically and guilty of minor infractions are read aloud for detention classes after school hours.

The proceedings entered the final sequence dramatically intoned by the headmaster's solemn voice announcing the names of students guilty of serious offenses before a hushed assembly. Names scrolled onto a ledger book with a black cover referred to as a "Black Book" was a record of offenders to be punished with seven strokes of a cane.

Five offenders were summoned, identified by their family names followed by the initial letter of a first name.

"Plummer L., for wearing a felt hat after many warnings."

"Williams A., for getting three detentions."

"Provident V., for wrongful possession and violence."

"Lambert F., for using foul language."

"Greaves M., for causing damage to school property."

The student's first name was rarely revealed or enunciated and was more often denoted by its initial letter. The preferred use of family names, customarily West European in derivation, was a subtle erasure of a past heritage and promoted assimilation. It also carried the expectation of students to uphold respectfully the family name hoping this would be reciprocated with family involvement in the student's conduct and performance. However, students were inclined to use pseudonyms they deemed suited to physical aspects and interests peculiar to them

"I refused to cry," Victor now in his fourth year at the school announced to his three friends Martin, Vivian and Thomas waiting on him in the schoolyard for a firsthand account of a punishment most students assiduously avoided.

"You okay, did it hurt?" Martin inquired mildly.

"He made me bend over and gave me six lashes and told me it was for my violent behavior," Victor said before pausing. "At one time, I felt like taking the cane from him and lashing him back."

"Boy don't ever try that, they will expel you from school," warned an alarmed Vivian who suggested an alternate strategy,

"Maybe we can corner Zane, that ass. I know where he hangs out."

"Yes, because that is not fair. Zane lash you with his ruler first and you took it from him but didn't even hit him back," said Martin who admitted, "Is because I said you saw him in Baxter's Yard behind the Janie girl."

"You see those stupid jokes you always making and putting people in trouble," Vivian scolded.

"Boy, you better don't let your father know," warned Thomas.

It was not unusual for parents to endorse the headmaster's decision for penalizing their sons as a reason for applying further punishment and assumed it was warranted.

"My father would skin me alive if he ever heard I got a caning," said Martin Innocent. His father Lennox used this expression frequently but Martin interpreted it to mean firm punishment.

However, Mrs. Innocent learned that her son's friend Victor received a caning from a nephew also attending St. Teresa College.

As Martin walked through the door after school, his Mother confronted him. "Martin, I do not want you to follow Victor. He is from a different background; you must look up, not down. I understand he was punished with a caning today."

"Ma, why you worry about me? The most I ever get is a detention. That priest, if I tell you he want to make everyone afraid of him, which is why Victor had to tell him don't say things that not true. Right away he gives the man a Black Book for that."

11

News of Victor's Black Book and caning leaked to his mother while attending a meeting of the Sacred Heart Fraternity in the company of Martin's mother. The two matriarchs were discussing the travails of bringing up children in the world of today.

"His father does not spare the rod if he misbehaves, and this policy has helped Martin to be a disciplined student," Martin's mother insisted.

"Well, my Victor, no matter what people say about the boys from Baxter's Yard, he set the best example and nobody not even his father never had to touch him."

Mrs. Innocent held her tongue for a moment then with an impromptu melody sang: "Father Limos doesn't think so, Father Limos doesn't think so."

The door of the Provident family hut slammed louder than usual after Herman walked in and the vibration alerted the household to an impending furor.

"I understood you got a Black Book?" Herman Provident threw the comment at his son studiously engaged in class homework. "Why do you want to disgrace your family? Here we are working hard to give you what we never had. Is that how you are showing your thanks?"

Victor did not reply immediately. He was aware of the futility of trying to defend himself against the robed ones who had travelled many miles to inculcate the philosophies of good and bad. "Father Limos don't like me."

"How you mean, he don't like you?"

"The other boys doing more things than me and is only me he sees deserve a Black Book."

"What more things is that? It is not for you to judge what Father Limos decide. All you have to do is behave your damn self. Boy, I cannot afford to pay for your school if Miss Mable hear of your bad behavior."

"I don't like him to bawl at me as if I am his dog."

"You know why? It is because he has to speak to you a hundred times before you does listen."

"No Daddy, not true, when it is Vivian or Thomas, he just says, 'quiet please.' Whenever he meets them is, 'How is your father and mother' and sends regards."

"So what has that got to do with you? These are well-to-do people. Although I am not in their class, Father Limos spoke to me well at registration, you know."

Victor looked down at the book as he rued his father's acknowledgment of his social status. A Catholic ordained "Father" was more pertinent to the direction of youth affairs than biological fathers of African origin. Herman believed the actions and decisions of Catholic priests always carried the imprimatur of the church. They were able to trace and document their histories over many generations and significantly to biblical times. Herman could not trace his ancestral past, but was unabashed in extrapolating from Judaea Christian philosophy a fable of African civilization.

"Don't listen to all these people who talking their nonsense about how the white man take them from Africa. I am happy He took us because God meant it to happen that way, so we could learn about Him. That is how He works His mystery."

12

Claire Beaufrand was considered to be among the prettiest girls on the island. She was an adorable belle with an angelic face, an hourglass shape, a nice tan and good hair, with the added chic, Parisian style of her French mother. As a local beauty, she could choose from the best of available suitors, but was in a quandary having to choose between the athlete and the academe, both high on the popularity index in their respective fields.

Thomas Blyth and Vivian Keswick were actually close friends each with their niche of popular achievement. Separately, they represented the two most sought after roles and revered disciplines of the school. Tom outdoor, Viv indoor; Tom athletic, Viv academic; and so it went, extrovert vs. introvert; Tom won many sporting trophies; Viv excelled in exams and accumulated certificates. The comradeship between Tom and Viv was promoted as an ideal of the school spirit and both served as role models for the newly established Catholic secondary school.

Claire's challenge was to bask in the amorous approaches of both graduating students without disrupting the exclusive bond between the suitors. Equally challenging was her quest for a tolerance for opposite gender friendships while attending St. John's Convent run by the Sisters of Our Lady of Sorrows whose vows of celibacy advocated strict separation of facilities for boys and girls.

The convent was a high-walled complex intended to be a bastion of chastity. The suppression of physical attributes was foremost in the design and style of the school uniform. There was to be no sign or prominence or attractiveness and to this end belts were to be loose fitting at the waist to lessen the protuberance of body parts.

Mother Superior, on occasion, expressed her concern following an average result on a midterm exam by Claire, a consistent "A" student.

"Claire, perhaps you need to pay more attention to your studies."

"I was not feeling well that day," offered Claire dryly.

"Is something the matter?"

"No, I am okay now."

"The reason I asked this is because I am receiving reports you are seen very often in the company of boys."

"Oh!" exclaimed a startled Claire. "Sometimes it is not my fault they would come around even when I am playing with other girls."

"I know, I can understand. This is why I am asking you to be careful especially as you have the ability to be a leader."

Claire had been made aware of her attractiveness by her peers and now this was proving to be a burden. She mulled over the reasons to keep away from boys or maybe just circumvent the matter without alarming persons. She sidled away from Mother Superior with a wry smile and commented.

"People sometimes say things just to impress you, especially if they believe you are listening to them."

"I do not believe they would have brought these matters to my attention if you were not seen wearing shorts in public," added Mother Superior.

Claire and the classmate she was walking with resumed their stroll across the Roman tiled courtyard uninterrupted and headed to the chapel for morning prayers.

"Imagine," began Claire, "people are telling Mother they see me often with boys."

"So what? Girl, if I was in your place, I won't worry about Mother. God gave you your looks that boys like and if they like to be with you so what?" argued Lynette.

"But guess what? They reported me to her for wearing shorts when a few of us went hiking to the lighthouse."

"You should have asked her if she wanted you to wear that stupid school uniform everywhere you go," Lynette said mockingly.

The function of the school uniform designed to suppress appearances that may be alluring to the opposite sex had markedly different results when observed on the externals of Claire and Lynette. For instance, Claire's hips curved out below the slackened belt and the outline of her breast protruded noticeably beneath the high apron covering her shirt blouse while no body part of Lynette extended beyond the extensive girth of her waistline.

Every girl attending school at the convent was tutored as a potential novitiate. Relationships with the opposite sex were restricted except in the context of brothers of the same family. Chastity was presented in a setting of concealment. Bodies were cloaked, unseen and untouched in an expression of virtue. The student psyche was constantly alerted to a common menace of their body in danger of being violated.

"To me it makes no sense to be born with a body and then have to cover it up with all this cloth," Lynette argued.

"Their bodies never conceived a baby or were ever pregnant, so why are they still hiding in their old age?"

Lynette tilted her head back and let out a giggly screech over Claire's comment and her eyes made unintended contact with the statue of the Virgin Mary prominent above the main entrance to the chapel. She grabbed Claire's arm bringing her to a standstill before entering the chapel. "The gown on the statue is the same as the nuns are wearing," observed Lynette pointing with her finger.

"You only just realize that?"

"Somehow my mind saw them existing in a different time, long, long ago."

In the chapel, a group of girls wearing different style and color uniforms sat together as in some sect with special rites of passage. Although the nuns made no formal announcement to the main student body about the distinction, the relevant reason was well known and had been filtered and tempered to teenage understanding. There were no more than a dozen of those students attending classes sticking together with behavior hesitant and unwelcoming and seemingly with misgivings about their surroundings. This Lynette believed hindered a closer relationship with a student she had tried to befriend. She referred the matter to her enlightened friend for a discerning opinion.

"I was speaking to one of the girls in the dark blue uniform and she sounds very intelligent."

"Surprise, surprise," responded Claire with a hint of sarcasm.

"But why should they have to wear a different uniform because they are born out of wedlock?"

"You are not supposed to have a child unless you have received the sacrament of matrimony."

"So if it is that simple, how is it they still were able to have a child."

Claire gave Lynette a look of frustration but Lynette continued.

"Yes, I know you have to have some sort of permission through the sacraments but how does that make them different from other children."

"They are born out of a sinful relationship."

"Yes, but you still haven't answered my question. How are they different and why have a separate school and classes for them?"

"The wages of sin."

"Born in sin should be borne by the parents not the children. I don't find they are any different from us."

13

The families of Claire, Lynette and Vivian owned mansions beyond the borders of Tabor City. Other stately residences of the wealthiest set were perched at various height levels on the periphery with a view of Tabor City and the church spire at its center. Residences of the next income levels were a few steps down toward the city center. They were families of Tom Blyth and Zane Carter that had withdrawn to the city perimeter after vacating neighborhoods next to the seaside that transformed into variable shoreline activities providing berthing facilities for schooners and coastal boats.

However, some neighborhood pockets in Tabor City had been able to maintain quiet seclusion although no part of the city was restricted. The citizens were respectful when walking in that vicinity and tipped their hats politely to greet residents leaning out of ground floor windows and when encountering prominent persons.

There was the street along which every funeral procession traveled to an intersection a few blocks away. On arriving there, the final blessing would be administered by a vested priest who was leading the procession accompanied by three acolytes. Walking directly behind the cortege were immediate family members followed by attending sympathizers separated by gender, the women walking ahead of the men in a convention observed by the retinue at most Catholic processions. Shops and homes along the route closed windows and doors every time a funeral cortege passed in front of their building in an apprehensive show of respect for the dead.

Some opulent family houses next to encroaching ghetto communities were adapting new strategies of survival. A high birth rate among the lower income residents had crept up to engulf the residences of Mable and Diana Baxter and others whose relatives had dispersed to new suburbs and oversea destinations.

Strange visitors from unfamiliar countries seeking modest accommodation appeared unobtrusively on island at any time of year presumably checked in by immigration officers who disinterestedly stamped their documents and routinely asked how long they intended to stay on the island.

In contrast, there was much interest by the hostesses of the Baxter and Williams' houses with their spare rooms to accommodate boarders, which provided a welcome source of income. The expertise for quick and accurate assessment of character had to be acquired to accept a diverse list of guests requesting accommodation for an overnight stay and beyond.

Mr. Hakim Mansur was the longest boarder on record at the Baxter House and had been a tenant for the last two years. He had since become an established member of the household and participated in the vetting of applying tenants. A source of apparent tension in the household was developing between Miss Mable and Hakim Mansur in resentment to Hakim's amorous attention to her sociable sister, Diana.

"So when I opened the door," Miss Mable mimed with her hand and extended her neck out the side window, "all I could see was Hakim's huge nose, the biggest nose I have ever seen in my life. All I could see was a Pinocchio in front of me."

At the window opposite, Nurse Grace giggled at Miss Mable's revulsion to the large nose of her tenant and burst into laughter when Miss Mable said, "He looked as if he was smelling whatever he was looking at and it seemed so unmannerly."

"I can imagine, but look now you hardly notice it," suggested Grace.

"No not even now, it still haunts me. I did not want to take him in because I," Miss Mable paused while someone passed between the houses at the entrance to the Yard. "Yes," she went on. "I was telling you I had already told him I had no room. But maybe I shouldn't tell you this."

"Since when you feel you cannot tell me something?" protested Nurse Grace.

"Well, let me continue, so Hakim was already going away, but then last minute he turns around with this big suitcase, opens it, and guess what?"

"I can hear him saying, plenty nice clothes, no like dress, no sleep in nice nighty," mimicked Nurse Grace.

"My sister happened to be there when I was interviewing him and you know how my sister likes clothes."

"Is not only clothes. I believe she like man more than the clothes," interjected Nurse Grace. Miss Mable reacted with a swift withdrawal from the window and slammed the shutters closed.

"Eesalop!" exclaimed Nurse Grace as the window slammed shut. "Imbecile! Hypocrite!" she yelled in further denunciation of her neighbor.

Retreating behind the closed window, Miss Mable was furious. She considered the remark injudicious. A dark curtain cloth to ward off any further intrusion was added days later.

14

The sacristan of the Roman Catholic cathedral had recently retired due to ill health or perhaps having aged beyond her eightieth birthday. As a calling, it ranked high among occupations from which a resignation would not be forthcoming as working in the temple offered fitting in-service preparation for the afterlife.

Mable Baxter was the assistant sacristan and performed with a dedication that was to assure her of promotion to head sacristan. For some time past, she performed the mundane responsibilities of ensuring the cleaning of the church, locking doors, extinguishing candles after the mass, making the pastry for the communion wafers, laundering and caring of all church vestments. However she longed for the more hallowed tasks at the inner sacristy to experience contact with the sacred vessels, such as filling the ciborium with a requisite number of wafers and the pitcher with wine, the placement of the chalice inside the tabernacle and other preparatory functions at the altar central to the Eucharistic mass. She wore in spinster fashion, ankle-length plain dresses as complementary regalia to the robed celibacy of officiating priests.

Persons responsible for organizing church ceremonies and religious events were highly respected in the community that on occasions was marked by self-righteous posturing and was possibly helpful to Miss Mable when collecting rental fees from her tenants.

Every Saturday, collections of rent from Baxter Yard tenants were fraught with disputes, alternating in cautionary reprieves and threats of eviction. Lynette was spending the weekend with her aunt and fascinated by the interaction remarked, "Auntie Mae, they act as if they are scared of you."

"That is all a pretense."

"Why do they pretend?"

"Ah my dear child, they are trying to make me drop my guard."

"What will happen if you drop your guard?"

"Observe those who pay show no sign of fear."

"So those who do not have the money pretend they are scared."

"That's right, my child. But they are the treacherous ones."

"Why, have they ever threatened or harmed you?"

Miss Mable gently clutched the cross that was attached to the chaplet hanging around her neck, "My child, if you believe and have faith, He will protect you."

A gate opened onto a corridor along the side of the building and served as the entrance for housemaids and tradesmen. On rent collection days, the gate swung open regularly and scraped the stony path underneath causing it to vibrate and jingle the bell attached to the back of the gate. Halfway along the path was a side door entrance where Miss Mable sat at a small table receiving monies from her tenants.

"Good morning to all," the shrill voice of Iris startled Mable and her niece Lynette.

"Iris, where did you pass?"

"I come by the gate, Miss Mable."

"How is it I didn't hear the bell? Iris, this is not the first time you appeared and I did not hear the bell."

"Miss, the bell knows is me and have no need to warn you." Lynette giggled.

"You use the little bit of strength you have left to lift my gate and sneak in last as usual. I hope today you have all the rent, sneaking in late not going to help this time." Miss Mable was exposing the ruse of Iris for Lynette's appreciation.

"I never see the trade so slow. All I sell today is a few packs of chewing gum, but God bless your soul 'cause I would be sleeping on the sidewalk if it were not for your good heart."

"While you are not responsible for anybody but yourself, a tray of knick knacks cannot support you and pay the rent."

"Miss Mable, I would be able if I didn't have Winifred who always sick on my hands, and I have to spend all my time helping her. I so vex. Winifred and I say who live longer responsible to bury the one who die first. Well, the other night she thought she was dying and a neighbor son come to call me after midnight but it was only a bad bellyache she had."

"Serve you right, and who is going to bury you if she die before you?"

Iris bent her head slightly with a smile of endearment.

"Don't smile for me; the nuns have a home for people with no relatives. You better book a space there."

Iris was shrewd at appeasing her landlady when upbraided for her arrears of outstanding rent and exploited an appreciation for her role as an exemplary and frequent churchgoer of the Baxter's Yard community. She impersonated Miss Mable with her prim spinsterish attire and pent up aggression. Iris walked with quick taut steps beneath the stiff mainspring of her upper body, coiled and ready to strike in tandem with her hostile glances. Now, restrained and suppliant before Miss Mable, she nimbly deflected the topic of outstanding rental.

"There is no better Auntie than you to guide this young mind. Every time I see her she has grown some more," Iris said, addressing Lynette directly. "If you listen to your Auntie you will not go wrong. Help your Auntie by getting me some water to drink, please, please, please."

As Lynette moved to get the water, Iris stepped closer to the table and her facial expression switched to alarm mode.

"Miss Mable, the big warship, they call the Frobisher just arrive in the harbor. The same one that was here some months ago with plenty sailors. You remember how Janie and Mabel bring all of those drunk sailors in the Yard with her friends? I know you complain plenty, but do you know they were even knocking on my door by mistake? You see what can happen. Well I see your brother child here, you cannot let her witness what can happen, too, too much bad behaving example for her if —"

Lynette returned humming loudly to alert Iris, who was crouched in a hush-hush pose, and handed her the glass of water.

"Thank you darling; on your wedding day."

"That will not be in the near future," Lynette assured.

"Enough, Iris. If I am not back from my brother tonight, keep an eye on the place for me."

Lynette expressed surprise, puzzled by the uneasiness and frowned inquiringly at her aunt as she hurriedly began preparation for their move to the suburban home of her brother.

"What's going on, Aunty? You look like you have got into a state over something."

"What makes you think so? I am in the habit of making quick decisions. I am going to put some clothes together to take with me."

As Miss Mable left the room Lynette turned sharply to Iris, "What did you tell my aunty that made her suddenly want to leave?"

"Me, we were talking about the good things in having family. It seems we always talk about that and this time it was all because of you."

"What about your family? Are they here on Au Tabor?" Lynette threw out the question with some misgiving.

Iris shook her head without emotion. "You know I wish I had."

"Do you know people around here think you are a mysterious person?" a probing Lynette continued.

"Is none of their business, all they do is mind people business, those ragamuffins and, and — your aunty does call them immoral, I don't keep company with them."

In a voice now filled with emotion, Iris asked, "Do you want to hear my story? I wish there were more people of your type I can talk to."

"Of course. I like hearing strange stories," encouraged Lynette with a wry smile.

"Well, I am an only child of parents who settled here from another island. My parents met as children growing up in an orphanage. They came here to escape a past, which according to my father had too many empty spaces, you understand, no mother and father. Their plan was to have many children to fill those empty spaces. However, this was not to be as my mother died as a result of my coming into this world. She gave me her space." Iris sighed aloud and then continued. "My dear, there are no empty spaces, there is no such thing as an empty space because they are all filled with wishes and dreams, and so it is better if you use your years making space so there is room for the things you want in this world."

Lynette stared vaguely attempting to make sense or derive lessons from the surprising tutorial but was hurried by her aunt to get ready to leave.

15

The town was teeming with white men in white tunics. They appeared on every street, at every corner in like outfits.

An alcoholic degenerate displayed his verbal skills and hailed the sailors as "vertebrate swarms of a maritime genus," and got a meaningless wave.

The mood in the town was amenable to the presence of the hulking all grey battleship HMS Frobisher with its all male crew. Advanced technology and a crew with superior skills heightened the local inferiority complex as this naval behemoth conquered mind, body and subjected territory of Au Tabor to an overseas kingdom.

However, there was no deterring of Raymond and Felix loitering on the waterfront among the many unwelcome loiterers claiming to be all round service providers. Raymond made the observation of certain tasks being performed by the white crew traditionally done in Au Tabor by locals. "Dese fellas bareback in the hot sun. You can see dey not happy cleaning and polishing and shining things."

"You think they will give us the job if we say we can do it for not much money?" a hopeful Felix inquired.

"Maybe, but the best thing is to come with everything ready to shine and take over right away," Raymond advised.

"Yeah, yeah, good idea. Okay, you will shine the brass things and I will shine the silver ones," proposed Felix.

They were confident such low level tasks would be passed on to them, so off to the shop they went, and out of their meager resources Raymond purchased a tin of Brasso and Felix a tin of Silvo.

It was not possible to negotiate privately while dozens of like characters were swarming around offering the sailors escort and other unrelated services. Despite their best efforts and assurances of sterling service, the offer was not accepted for reasons ranging from safety and security measures to lack of skills. Raymond and Felix became very upset after making themselves available with cleaning materials, a rag of used clothing and a jingle.

"We shine brass or silver, expert shine all over for brass and silver."

While standing on the dock their behavior over the disappointment deteriorated into insults and invective hurled loosely at the entire crew of the warship. They were later apprehended by police for threatening the store clerk when making a bogus claim that the tins of polish were mistaken items purchased for someone. The clerk had refused to accept the return of the tins of Brasso and Silvo for a refund of the purchase price.

From then on, they were subjected to the pastime of taunts from bystanders who found playful delight in teasing the two pretenders. Mention of the jingle in their presence or calling out 'Raymond Brasso' would result in a street chase or a stone throwing attack while a shout of 'Felix Silvo' resulted in a lengthy spewing of foul language and verbal abuse.

The island's football team was given a merciless drubbing of six goals to nil by the Frobisher's elite football team adding further diminution to the island's pride and causing two ardent fans, Alticor and Primus, much distress and to have an exchange of views.

"Man if you have to compare, it look like a warship stronger than the whole island," observed Alticor.

"Because dey can beat us at football, dat not making sense for you to say dat," Primus countered.

"Okay, den tell me one ting. Where you tink we better dan dem?"

"What you expect? Dese men are from a big country. Dey see and know a lot more tings dan us. Dey training everyday not only to fight wars but to play football too and now dey here just to play, relax and take time off."

"Den we should make the island like one big battleship and train everybody on it," Alticor suggested.

"Maybe if we did not have women and children. You know the battleships don't have to worry wid dat?"

"True, very true. Only when they land here they does see women."

"At least we good for one ting."

"Check dat out, if we organize a big sailor mas-band in time for carnival and de warship arrive same time and confuse tings, boy wha you tink will happen?" Alticor presented what he thought was a possible dilemma.

"Man, why you so stupid? So you goin meet dem wid rowboat and tell dem de town already busy wid one set sailor band so remain offshore? Boy, dey go pelt two canon in your backside." Primus knocked down the supposition aggressively.

"But in my own island."

"Boy you dunno who ruling you, you tink you is in Africa. Better hurry go lock your woman inside before it too late."

Nighttime saw an even larger impact of the sailors on the town as the local populace retired indoors with the exception of entertainers and ladies with associated pimps plying sexual favors for undisclosed gain.

"Sailors in drunken stupor wobbled out of alleyways and ramshackle bars, propped and guided by women hooking their arms in seeming captivity and surrender. "Feeling lonely? Look like you need some company. I can show you a good time."

It could be assumed the crewmembers of the HMS Frobisher were granted a broad exemption by the local constabulary. Although there was some evidence of naval police, attempts to curb the unruly behavior were hardly noticeable and free rein seemed to have been allowed given the smashing of glass bottles, occasional fights and indecent language.

The dark of night has always been blamed for nocturnal malediction and so all good people stayed indoors to escape the obscenity, terror and dread as the visitors reveled in the uncontested freedom of nighttime.

Many of the residents of Baxter's Yard undergo extreme anxiety hoping the vagaries of such activity do not escalate out of control. Those residents with reservations would not even have given thought to protesting fearing they would incur the wrath of a sizeable number of residents catering to the unanticipated source of income. They also could not expect support from the authorities whose only likely contribution to the war effort was to offer the island as a recreational facility.

Herman and Lorna closed every opening to the outdoors and assembled the children. Herman held their attention spinning folktales. The children giggled oblivious of the obscenity.

16

The morning return of innocents could be seen entering church doors as dawn's light crept up from behind the surrounding hills. And even though it was Sunday, the street cleaners were sweeping up the garbage and debris of unnamed polluters. However there were no morally cleansing petitions, no condemnation of the acts of debauchery or a sermon of reprimand. Only the trash being foraged by scrawny curs remained as evidence of the night's events.

Among the earliest returnees to town were Miss Mable having tacitly approved the recreational night for the gallant defenders of the empire. With her niece Lynette, she had absconded to the safe haven of her brother's home and now the sacristy of the church was given priority to ensure all systems for church services throughout the day were in place. She was eventually beset by Lynette.

"You still have not told me why you hurried to daddy's home and stayed overnight," Lynnette said.

"You ask too many questions, my dear child."

"Aunty, last night you said you would explain in the morning. You promised."

"People can have a change of mind sometimes"

"I believe something made you afraid."

"Afraid? Me, no-no!"

"Something Iris whispered to you got you afraid."

"Why do you think so?"

"You told me some of them were treacherous."

"And didn't I tell you I have my faith and it protects me?"

"By the way, you should not keep all that rent money here." Lynette, wanting to be taken seriously, offered a lesson on security.

"Don't worry. I have a lifelong experience and knowledge of those people."

The bow section of HMS Frobisher could be seen from the balcony upstairs of the Baxter home. A view of sailors lined up in drill formation on the deck was opportune to overcome any misgivings and enlighten Lynette where her heritage and loyalty lay or so Aunty Mae hoped.

"Lynette, come this side to see this."

"Just now, Aunty?"

"Hurry up."

When Lynette joined her in the balcony, she pointed to beyond the roofs of neighboring houses.

"There is our protection. See the discipline of these men. They protect us from the enemy and ensure our safety. God save the King."

Lynette stared impassively in the direction of the ship and reckoned its presence to be at the obvious harbor location alongside the wharf. Her guardians were unwavering in protecting her wellbeing; choosing the convent and its spiritual surround of stone-faced images guarding her against evil and now the navy ship with massive weaponry protecting her material welfare. All this Lynette reflected on as being remote from her foremost longings.

17

Two years after the war, ceremonial activity and commemoration of wartime events such as remembrance wreath laying and honor parades occurred regularly as the surplus of uniformed personnel were no longer on active duty.

The first Saturday of the month of June was always designated a public holiday in honor of the birthday of the reigning King George VI. It was always a prestigious day for local English born residents. The year was 1946 and celebrations for the monarch began with the usual pomp of a parade on the public square in the morning. The visit of the HMS Frobisher was planned to coincide with the birthday celebrations and provide added attraction to the year's parade. The St. Teresa's College Cadet Corp led by Cadet Sergeant Major Thomas Blyth marched in fourth place behind the police.

A contingent of sailors off the warship paraded along with every brigade unit established on the island by Britain. Another addition to the roster that year was the St. Johns Ambulance Brigade and also marching four abreast were four women from the military unit of the soon to be disbanded Women's Auxiliary Territorial Service (A.T.S.) unit. They were a dwindling elite group of ladies who felt a profound need to support the troops in militaristic style and demonstrated an all gender character to the war effort.

Perhaps another contributing motive was privileged access to the eligible male counterparts who formed the local branch of the West India Army Regiment. However this branch was disbanded soon after the war ended and a social club image seemed to be replacing the military profile.

Apparently the local citizens of Tabor were not made aware the warship HMS. Frobisher would be giving a 21 gun salute on His Majesty's birthday, so the first blast of the canon sent hearts pulsing at a panic stricken pace and momentarily froze all bodily function.

Not so, however, with scores of terrified stray dogs racing at maximum speed away from their favorite waterfront hangout as though heading to an uptown dog-fest. There were the scrawny, the disabled, the injured on three legs, all gave up mating encounters, scavenging and dogfights. It was a source of great amusement among locals although themselves, having just recovered their normal breathing rhythm after the heart stopping canon blast.

Some members of the St. John's Ambulance contingent had to give attention to a usual list of fainting participants. One cadet, two scouts and a girl guide fainted in cinematic fashion, supinely at attention, fortunately onto a lush grass surface. The second half of the groups parading were out of step to the barely audible beat of the police band a few hundred yards ahead.

Later that evening at 6:30 pm at Government House was the gathering of the crème de la crème of society attending a birthday reception for King George V1.

Vivian's father, Dr. Richard Keswick, and wife, Dora, joined the queue at the entrance to the gala hall and after perfunctory handshakes of welcome by the resident administrator, they met with other dignitaries.

The police band was playing calypsos in a marching tempo and the bandmaster conducted with a prance in his step on the podium.

A specific request on the invitations for tonight's reception encouraged the wearing of national or ceremonial dress and medals. The perennially gowned clerics of religion, those outfitted in traditional garments of their profession and nationality along with officers of HMS Frobisher in their white naval uniforms complimented the stately setting and imperial ambiance of the gala hall.

Unexpectedly, the stentorian voice of uniformed Colonel William Blyth, Tom's father, intruded on a conversation between Dr. Keswick and four other invited guests.

"Richard, are you among the medals tonight?"

Tall, militarily handsome, the picture perfect loyalist, Colonel Blyth of the defunct West India Regiment was among the redundancies of the Second World War and was at the time reclaimed in the post as chief of the local police force. He preferred the uniform of a former army colonel. He paraded that morning with the police contingent in a white jacket and black trouser tunic but the evening was outfitted in British colonel khaki. Without his military headdress, the elegant profile was slightly compromised by a balding head which, when covered, offered no suggestion of alopecic deficiency.

The question infuriated Dr. Keswick. Other invitees within earshot were attentively awaiting a response.

"As an officer who I assume is steeped in protocol, why not await the answer when availed from an appropriate source," snapped Richard Keswick.

Those pausing to eavesdrop acted disinterestedly except Colonel Blyth who smartly introduced a change of subject, "By the way

Richard, something I have wanted to discuss with you."

Those previously engaged in conversation with Dr. Keswick mingled into other groupings. "I have been receiving reports not surprisingly on the behavior of a student out of Baxter's Yard named Victor who is closely associated with your son. Needless to say, I have warned my son to exercise caution in relation to him."

"Fortunately, I have no intention. Or, should I say, he will not be entering a military academy and so I expect his behavior will not be given to a ranking in status among friends."

Dr. Keswick signaled for a drink and walked to the waiter in a determined attempt to create some distance between himself and William Blyth.

18

Relative calm followed the end of the world war and was timely for new religious outreach to the colonies. Catholic institutions with their complement of clergy and lay workers arrived on Au Tabor to conduct spiritual retreats and enhance already established missions in Catholic education. Roman Catholicism was espoused as the authentic church and religion based on its proven lineage from the Apostle, Saint Peter. The faithful were cautioned to partake of the sacraments administered by ordained clergy to attain divine goodness and redemption. The human exemplars of goodness in the most hallowed state were French, Irish and Belgian clergy of Caucasian ethnicity.

A wave of new procedures was being implemented by the churches' administrators to coincide with the elevation of the parish to an archdiocese, and also the honor of having its own resident bishop. The formats for worship and other religious ceremonies were being amended to suit widening ripples of lower class parishioners who are wiping out privileges of reserved pews, silencing the preferential toll of church bells and eliminating unnecessary sinecures. Child baptisms and sacramental rite previously performed at the entrance door for the underprivileged had now moved closer to the main altar.

Churches, convents, and presbyteries occupied prime space in the center of towns and villages. They were central in many ways to life on the island as prominent symbols of civic and moral authority. In the rural districts, stone temples and edifices of worship were externally dominant and imposing with interiors rich in ecclesiastical ornament. The virtue of humility, a fundamental tenet of the church, was symbolized ironically by Lilliputian huts with straw, shingle and rusting zinc roofs meekly squatting around the massive church structures. These structures appeared to be replicas of the temples and basilicas as are found in Rome and were built largely with labor of village folk before and after the era of slavery.

Generally, the populace of Au Tabor remained loyal to the religion into which they were baptized and were later required to follow instruction for their salvation. At every station, they inevitably faced a moral dilemma when creature instincts battled religious commandments amid fears of extinction and loss of temporal pardons.

The Colonial Office department of the United Kingdom ran the government and treasury of Au Tabor and took responsibility for maintaining its physical infrastructure. It noticeably assigned other vital functions to the Catholic establishment and also tailored many important social policies in line with church principles and rules. Divorce, for example, was outlawed.

The United Kingdom had conceded to the island's three major religious bodies - Catholic, Anglican and Methodist - all of the island's educational needs including teachers, and the physical structure of school buildings. Nevertheless, most of the ethical and moral codes were in keeping with Roman Catholic religious philosophy and beliefs.

With few exceptions, public holidays were based on the Catholic liturgical calendar and Roman law. The Catholic establishment had always been arguably the largest provider of school places at both primary and secondary levels and consequently exercised considerable influence on educational policy matters.

All the while church and state had been coexisting and collaborating on policy involving the management of the island's educational system and appeared to be administered along high moral standards and policy accord. The assistance of the churches in providing teachers and other infrastructural facilities contributed to budgetary savings for the state and in turn provided the churches with a helpful recruiting platform. As this partnership became secure, Roman Catholic parents were coerced to send their children to Catholic schools or chance being denied certain religious privileges. This action contributed to a faultfinding rivalry among denominational institutions on the island.

Meanwhile, there was a major constitutional development. The United Kingdom granted a measured opportunity for Au Tabor citizens to be elected to form part of the island's administration and so aspire to political office. However, this latest concession was that incomes of candidates and voters alike must not fall below a specified amount. The political aspirants sprang from two quarters, the legal fraternity and the trade union movement, which divided political rivalry between two groupings, legislative gurus and basic needs campaigners.

In the first instance, the legal and upper income candidates dominated because many persons likely to support trade union candidates fell below the qualifying income level.

Within a couple years, this minimum income requirement was overturned, giving every citizen 21 years and over voting rights.

The obvious conditions for true majority rule reversed the political landscape. Many who cut their teeth in the trade union movement were acquiring legal and other academic qualifications resulting in a sophistication of ideas in the leadership of the trade union movement. Signs of a strain began to appear in the relationship between the Catholic church and state as more persons with professional qualifications aspired to political office and some in the political chain of command were in an overt thrust to "modernize" the civil code into more mainstream socialist thinking.

Introducing new legislation that conflicted with status quo doctrine of the church was a politically risky exercise. An elected member responsible for the direction of educational policy had the temerity to suggest legislation limiting subsidies and other influences of the church over educational facilities and curriculum administration. In response an energized and powerful Catholic clergy was activated to oust from influential positions anyone expressing divergent views to those of the church and was ably supported by righteous gentry and influential citizenry.

The proposed controversial education bill found support from another member of the local parliament who was a self declared agnostic. During a debate on the subject in the legislature, his contribution, which angered the church authorities, stated, "We are newly presented with a doctrinal account of the universe luring us into a feeling of spiritual deficiency. We are persuaded to witness invisible legions of angels and seraphs in a delusional blindness that displaces knowledge of our own reality. Why are we being taught so fervently to embrace fear, hell and damnation, in conflict with our style of love and communal participation?

"The ownership of our bodies and souls is being challenged with yet another request for us to hand over control once more to a new set of cultural stewards. Won't they consign us as on previous occasions to their preferred place of promise if we throw ourselves into dependence on them? Now that we are free they want us back on the plantation carrying our free will with us this time."

The Catholic faithful rallied strongly in opposition with protest marches and candlelight vigils. The contribution by the agnostic infuriated all Christians on the island and was construed by the majority of the faithful as beyond sacrilege and to be viewed on the most extreme plane of heretical doctrine.

Those dissenters of the current structure of the island's school system were shunned and their persons brought into disrepute.

19

A growing estrangement in religious attendance by younger Catholics was interpreted by Catholic regional authorities responsible for ecclesiastical affairs on Au Tabor as a nascent desire for representation by local clergy. The result was a recruitment drive for novitiates from the community to train at a new seminary established on a neighboring island.

Despite militant opposition, the member of the legislative council was assuaged by the support for speaking out fearlessly even though the subject was controversial and his council seat depended on an aggregation of votes.

Intellectuals from other professional disciplines weighed in with eclectic statements like, "It was phenomenal; the dome of Rome had been lifted by a maverick parliamentarian who complained of the dirge in sultry rituals that should be replaced with our natural tropical variations."

There seemed to be no lessening in ferment of current theological disputes giving momentum to every Bible-toting, verse-and-chapter-quoting-charlatan. Sidewalk and street corner preachers each claimed to have deciphered the correct azimuth to heavenly glory. A few men whose professed aspiration was saving souls surprised many in Au

Tabor at the blatant travesty of spiritual instruction.

There was Mike's alias, "The Human Radio" a few coins scattered on a piece of cloth at his feet as a decoy and using a large cardboard cone to amplify his offer of celestial reservations.

"In my Father's house, there are many mansions, the rooms are prepared if, if you are prepared there is a room for you."

Casimir, accompanied by two sons assisting as readers and responders and collecting donations from bystanders, warned, "The last time the world was destroyed by water but you all learn to swim. Well let me tell you, the next time he will destroy it with fire."

Reverend Dandy, a mulatto and best dressed of the street side preachers was regarded as an unstable and incoherent pseudo intellectual.

"What opportunities are we cultivating for discovery and achievement, a confidence in the difference between living in a world and not doing anything to improve it – yes in your bloody sex driven minds, yes, remain there, remain there and you will see, he's coming down just now."

As a young boy in the community, Pastor Jonas was a former acolyte and the only one who assailed the Catholic Church directly.

"For those who tell me Christ was born in a manger and we celebrate and honor him wearing elaborate vestments and ornaments of gold."

Reverend Freddie came from a neighboring island to take part in a boxing competition ten years prior, and he was among the many residents that lingered until he blended into the diverse community of Baxter's Yard. Freddie was known for his needless boasting – always predicting he would knock out every opponent he faced. After every loss in the ring, he tried a new venture until lately he espoused religion as a panacea for all ills and hard luck.

"There is nothing God can't do if we pray hard, and I know of one way He might help the poor and feed the hungry!" shouted Pastor Freddie, suggesting a menu of miraculous conversion.

"For let's suppose He turn all the fishes in the sea into chunks o' pork, and all the stones in the sea into dumplings, and all the sea into soup, no problem after that."

Unhappily for Pastor Freddie, at that moment the boys from Baxter's Yard heard him on the way home from a football match and began heckling.

"Freddie, like you hungry; instead of fooling people, go work for a living Freddie you still knockout, Freddie the fake."

Basil was a robustly built preacher, threatening anyone in his roaming congregation who made fun of him. He never failed to end his preaching session with the warning.

"All you so who acting stupid, on the last day when I goin up sitting next to the Lord in his golden chariot, you goin shout, Basil, Basil gimme a lift but I goin look down and cuss you so bad, you hear."

20

A congregation's year-round genuflection was suspended for a tacit concession of two days hedonistic revelry described with incongruous aplomb as the "Lenten Carnival." However, a non-binding pledge extracted in return for sanctioning a heathen festival was designated as a sacrifice of forty days of fasting and abstinence after carnival Tuesday or as at the commencement of Ash Wednesday.

"And oh the carnival, there is nothing like it," Grace excitedly related to Hakim. She was unrepentant in her joy.

"This is one time I really have fun," Grace continued. "It don't matter if I am not in disguise or costume. When the music start and everybody breakaway, you would never believe it's me. Man I going to town." Then Grace showed Hakim an abbreviated version of her dancing when he sprang from his seat.

"Teach me how you do it," he pleaded with arms outstretched.

Grace quickly backed away. "I will show you at carnival time."

"I practice so I ready carnival time."

"Don't worry when you hear the steel band music and the ping-a-ling-a ling sound of iron, you will find yourself dancing without even knowing," Grace teased with another jig of her waist.

Hakim retreated to his chair but couldn't resist complaining. "I like visit you because everything is church by Miss Mable, but for you to make good friends no, no, always treat me bad, no dance with me."

"Hakim, what is a Pinocchio? Ma Baxter say when she first saw you, she thought it was a Pinocchio."

Hakim circumvented the question. "This lady have bad tongue, I will not tell many bad things she say about you, she try prevent me talk to you."

"Tell me, tell me, what she said," Grace pleaded.

"She just say you nobody before you marry big family."

"Tell her I work hard for what I have and I know what burning her."

"She not happy you live next to her. What mean class? She say low class, high class but I not understand."

"Tell me Hakim you see anything wrong with me why I can't have what she has."

"You young she old, you pretty she has ugly face, why you worry?"

Grace blushed with a quiet smile. "Hakim, do you want something to drink?"

"Tea please. Hot tea."

Grace was a widow. Her deceased husband was the only son of the prominent Justice Williams of the high court. Academically and socially the son never matched the prowess of his father. He married Grace after his parents who had initially frowned on the courtship but eventually did give up on resistance to the union.

Grace was born out of the Baxter's Yard environment and had limited birth credentials. It was alleged that her mother left the island when she was two years old, leaving her in the care of a friend and promising to return within two months. The specified time of return expired and to date her mother's destination and whereabouts remained unknown. All inquiries with reference to the fate of Grace's mother were directed to the surrogate who reaffirmed that she had attempted to extract more information from Grace's mother before her departure. Grace's mother promised a full account upon her return and related the only briefing received on the mission.

"She tell me she going to meet someone who she believe is her child father, but he don't want her to mention it to anyone or she could lose her chance for him to help her. So I felt happy for her and that is why I agree to keep the child for her in the meantime."

However, her whereabouts were still unknown after fourteen years. Whether she was alive was sometimes disputed among the folk of Baxter's Yard although they expressed little hope of finding sponsors to conduct an investigation. And so there was seldom a referral to the paternity of Grace Williams nee Jones and everyone remained clueless.

Grace began her working life at sixteen as a nursing aide and displayed a single minded and persistent yearning to reach goals many told her were beyond her ability. She eventually qualified as a registered nurse. While being true to her vocation, she received her marriage proposal three days after extending care to the proposer during his short stay for removal of his appendix.

A guarded relationship at the start turned to praise and admiration. Justice Williams, the father-in-law, of Nurse Grace said she was a godsend when his wife who was suffering from terminal cancer benefitted from the nursing care and services of a professional.

Grace was never legally a ward of her mother's friend who cared for her over the years. Her history was handled with the usual curiosity for this nuptial occasion but never with an investigative effort to fill in and account for her missing links. But her marriage plans were never in jeopardy and all papers received the approbation of the church given the status of the groom.

Grace was intent on returning the benevolent care to her loving foster caretaker, her mother's friend and adoptive parent. The opportunity was denied her unfortunately when her adoptive parent became ill and died soon after she began working.

Grace inherited the historic mansion of Justice Williams which upkeep and maintenance was a burden despite her supplementary income from accepting boarders.

Grace returned from the kitchen with the tea and straight away asked curiously,

"Tell me, I thought you were friendly to Miss Mable's sister, Diana?"

"She friend with me but I not friend with her," Hakim shot back.

A skeptical Grace was not prepared to accept Hakim's response. "You want me to believe all the nice things she wearing, you did not give it to her?"

"Sometime I give. I feel sorry because she not strong. Her sister control everything. Don't worry I bring more than that for you."

"Me, I have everything I need and I can always buy what I want. Furthermore, I didn't ask you for your things," Grace said, leaning towards Hakim to ensure her words reached his ears.

"Why you like that? I am kind person with good heart." Hakim looked genuinely.

"Your heart, your rent and your bed, all belong next door." Grace was not going to let up.

"I move now, now, I fix all damage in your house, stop roof leak and if you want I bring half of money to buy share in house so you have no worry." Hakim switched to an aggressive strategy to match Grace's stubborn stance.

"Just so Hakim," squealed Grace in surprise. "How we reach there? We are talking about carnival."

"I just show how heart can move over." Hakim sensed his offer made inroads and Grace was now defensive with her answers.

"Not so fast Hakim. If you want to join our carnival band, I have just the right part for you." Grace firmly powered the talk into new subject matter.

"What's that?" Hakim asked uncertain about the offer.

"Our band will be sugarcane cutters and you have the right color and looks to be the slave master with the whip."

"You crazy," snapped Hakim, as his face twitched in a semi-smile considering Grace could not be serious.

"C'mon, don't worry. It's carnival, anything goes."

"You want them kill me and then I have no business." He waved both hands signaling a firm no.

"Wha happen to you? Carnival is displaying what happened in the past, here and in other places, and it has nothing to do with the present."

"In my country, for bad past we pray never to happen again." Hakim joined his palms with this solemn overstatement and cynically asked, "But why you dance if it was not happy time?"

Grace listened having already decided nothing would interfere with her carnival preparations. She was not interested in chatting about the differences in cultural expression but instead sought material assistance.

"You just have to understand, it is mainly for the folks in the Yard. I organize this kind of band every year because they cannot afford fancy expensive costumes. You know what, help us with four yards of khaki to make slave master costume, we had already decided to make Victor the slave master and we will rub him all over with white lime."

21

At the first light of dawn in the city center, the elderly were extending their limbs in the restricted walking space of balconies while later in the day spinsters leant over the parapets or out of first floor windows and gossiped with passersby. The young debutantes responded cautiously to whistles and low voice intonations from courting young men through jalousie windows, chancing sometimes a quick glimpse. Paved sidewalks sheltered by balconies overhead were busy thoroughfares especially during the rainy season or to avoid the direct rays of the sun.

The home of favorite aunt, Mable, was favored by Lynette because of the loneliness she felt at the secluded suburban home of her parents. She often visited her religiously zealous aunt opting to sometimes spend the weekends with her and was engrossed by the raunchy chatter and boorish behavior of the occupants of Baxter's Yard. The only resident of the Yard known to her was Victor Provident, a school friend of Vivian Keswick whom she had met while recreating with Claire and Vivian.

Victor would casually recline for hours on a post supporting the Baxter house balcony when he knew Lynette would be there. No one connected her visiting days to his timely presence next to the entrance of the Yard.

Recently during breakfast Lynette introduced the name of Victor Provident with adulation for having achieved 'Victor Ludorum' at the school's athletic meet. He managed to edge out the popular favorite Thomas Blyth as the athlete with the highest aggregate of points based on the events in which they competed.

"Victor, the Victor Ludorum," gleefully announced Lynette, "Aunty you should be proud that a boy from Baxter's Yard won such an important trophy."

"He is a nice boy but you must have regard to his background and how he got there," pointed out her aunt Mae quietly between sips of coffee.

"Yes, isn't it great? Because of his background he has to walk many miles every day to school. That gave him stamina to win races."

Aunty Mae's eyes flickered on realizing Lynette missed the gist of her remark but chose not to comment further. Lynette had no idea she paid Victor's school fees.

Vivian and Thomas were hardly aware of Lynette when in the company of her best friend Claire and all attention and compliments were directed at Claire. Also Thomas made disgustingly personal remarks about Lynette's body using disparaging terms about her size and shape with claims that he could improve on her figure if she followed a regimen of exercise he would suggest. Lynette saw this as a form of retributive justice for Victor nipping past him as the top honor athlete and sent him a sympathy note, which read as follows:

Now you know what it feels like to be a wounded champion, I hope you will be kinder as a loser and realize everyone has feelings. I hope your ego has undergone a total makeover and developed respect for the Victor the Victor Ludorum; [I thoroughly enjoy the pun].

There was a measure of intended humiliation in the use of Victor as messenger. Thomas had a premonition the contents of the note would be unflattering anticipating retaliation to his jibes. He was tempted to not accept, but overcome with a desire to read Lynette's thoughts, he snatched the note from Victor's hand, glimpsed at the contents and thrust it back at him with the sneering remark:

"I would be lowering myself by accepting private communication from someone far below my social circle."

Victor stood motionless; his body reacted back and forth in dispositions of self-control and aggression. Never before had epithets of class or social discrimination aggrieved the solidarity of the gang of four and since it was without precedent, a stunned Victor could not work out a reason.

He looked briefly at the note in his hand, faulting its sender for the humiliating experience. The street intersection where he encountered Thomas was a block from the office of Thomas's father at police headquarters and incidentally the office was the intended place of delivery.

Unsavory feelings about class and image lingered with Victor as he walked hurriedly along familiar streets to his home. He began to evaluate the demeanor of everyone of comparable status for any suggestion of underlying snobbery. It angered him when he thought his father had succumbed or capitulated to discriminatory treatment at public institutions or did not receive due recognition accorded others. He had never considered a reaction beyond the feeling of anger and felt emboldened to ring the front door bell of Miss Mable's residence.

The door opened, Miss Mable and Victor stood facing each other, silent stares and no sign of welcome until. "I have a message for Lynette from Tom Blyth."

"Lynette someone is there to you," shouted Miss Mable still holding the doorknob with her head turned to direct her voice upstairs. When Lynette came bounding down the stairs in a sheer item of clothing, she got a sharp reprimand,

"Lynette, go back upstairs and put on a proper dress."

Lynette caught a glimpse of Victor on the step outside the opened door as she abruptly turned around in compliance. Meanwhile Miss Mable still with a hand on the doorknob spoke to Victor for the first time since opening the door, "What is the message?'

"Lynette gave me this note for Tom Blyth and I brought it back for her."

"Let me have it, I will pass it on to her."

Victor promptly handed over the note and right after the door closed.

22

A meeting of the Baxter's Yard carnival band was in progress at Grace's home comprising a self-appointed organizing committee of three persons, Nurse Grace, Janie and Victor. They were seated in the seldom-used living room. The baroque décor and period furniture required an upright seated position in a formal setting that implied restraint and minimum animation.

The business of the meeting was to be conducted in an informal manner and without an agenda, so it was no surprise when Grace began with a gossipy chat and suggestion. "The lady next door always quarreling about noise, so I hope when we start to practice our carnival act. But wait, maybe Victor you can ask her permission. I am sure this won't be the first time you find yourself at Ma Baxter front door."

"So you saw me?"

"Of course I saw you, you taking big chance going after the lady niece. Boy, you don't know your place."

"But Miss Grace, how you reach there, ask me what happen? Anyway, leave that alone. You say we will call the carnival band 'Cane Cutters of Au Tabor,'" Victor said.

"Yes, we already decide that but I waiting for you to tell me what happen?"

An irritated Victor ranted, "What you want to know for? You should be the last person to talk, you didn't know your place with the judge's son and you take chance and got big house."

"Boy, you have no respect for people older than you eh, but maybe that is why you will be a good slave master for our carnival band," Grace said taking umbrage.

"I don't see the connection." Victor said with a puzzled look.

"Your fastness and your big mouth is the connection, we going to cover your body with white lime, dress you in khaki with long socks and a panama hat and give you a whip," Grace spoke firmly to cover an explanation she knew didn't hold up.

"You know I have no long cheap dress like what the people from the country used to wear before," a concerned Janie interjected feeling left out and warned. "You only paying attention to slave master who is only one person and we have 50 others who have to dress up as the laborers."

Grace responded promptly with a full description, "That's easy, just wear one of your long nighties and put an ordinary dress over it, then you tie a big piece of string tight around your waist so your bottom sticks out and tie the handle of a tin cup to the string for when you want to fire one and after that wrap a piece of cloth around your head and tie it beneath your chin. Each person will have a long whole cane with the leaves still on it and pretend to be cutting cane. "

"You know something look for another slave master for your carnival band, I beating pan for carnival."

"You joining all those steel band ruffians who in a fight every carnival instead of coming with us. Boy, your father will be upset when he hear that," Grace warned hoping Victor would change his mind.

"You ever hear me in fight, and because those fellas behaving bad sometimes that doesn't mean I join them," claims Victor.

"And how is that you in trouble with the priest in school for fighting with Zane and insult the police chief son, what's his name, uh, Tom with a funny last name?"

"Why you fight with Zane?" Janie chimed in, suddenly interested.

"You didn't know the headmaster flog him for fighting with Zane?" Grace asked, turning to Janie before Victor could enter a defense.

"You believe you know everything that is happening. Hear what happen, they told Zane I said he always in the Yard behind you Janie, so he hit me with a ruler and I grab it from him but I never hit him back," Victor made clear.

"You see that, I told him I would come and meet him somewhere else and he should not come in the Yard."

"So if he always in the Yard behind you, that is true then, so why get vex?' queried Grace.

"Because what they thinking is not true. My father always gives him the money for me and believe me, that is the only reason why."

Grace and Victor looked at each other with a perplexed look of who was going to ask the next potent question. But Janie, sensing the puzzlement in the expressions, continued. "Maybe you all don't know Mr. Ronald Carter is my father. Zane is my half-brother you know."

Grace extended her eyelids and Vivian yanked his head to one side. There were more exchanges of glances until Grace sought final confirmation.

"Mr. Carter who plays the organ in church?"

"Uh huh, one thing you know Zane not ashamed to be my brother. He tell me he will always come straight to my door."

Victor was pensive in assessing and recalibrating his opinion of Zane.

"Surprise, surprise, maybe if I had known," Victor said finally, unsure whether he should continue.

In her usual blasé manner, Grace had a suggestion. "You know what? I will ask Zane to join our carnival band."

"You mad!" Victor's outburst drew a stare of alarm from Grace.

She remained silent as Victor went on. "Zane goes to church every morning. He is a very holy boy, the priests don't touch him even though he always failing his tests."

"Never mind dat. He is a good person, only sometimes he have a bad temper and is very thin-skinned. Let me tell you, once — "

Victor interrupted Janie to make his point.

"So you see I am not lying on him."

"Let me tell you. Once he came there and saw my boyfriend hitting me. He jump on the man and start to fight with him. Maybe my boyfriend was so surprised, he just stop and walk out."

"He should try and come more often to stop him from hitting you."

"Nurse Grace dat is why people never want you to know their business. You always adding what you want."

"So when you bawling the whole Yard down, I am adding? I am sure Victor hear you sometimes, eh Victor?"

"Come you all enough, when we going to call a meeting to tell everyone about the band, I know they waiting to hear from us," appealed Victor.

"Anyway, Zane tired tell me to leave that man and to move in with an old aunt of his dat living all by herself."

Janie ignored Victor's plea and was helped by Grace. "So why don't you move?"

"Me, to leave where I am, all my friends are here. When carnival time who go look for me. Furthermore I don't want any old lady to bother me."

"You rather stay in this place? You get a chance to move to a decent home with all the things, fridge, stove, running water inside the house."

"Nurse, you go come all the way up the road to take care of me if I sick, eh nurse?"

"Don't give me that, as long as you don't want to leave this damn man and you will not be able to bring him inside the house if you move up there."

"Nurse, I want to have a child," said Janie, this time her voice was soft and her eyes looked far away.

"You sure the man want a child and going to support it."

"Ay, ay Nurse I not making child to give to no man, I want my child for myself."

Victor clapped three times to make certain he had Grace and Janie's attention. They were getting off track.

"What's happening, what happen to the carnival meeting we suppose to be having? Was it just style to say we having carnival meeting?

"But you done spoil everything and say you not joining our carnival band," Nurse Grace complained.

Victor and Janie looked up at the ceiling distracted by the sound of footsteps on the floor above.

"Nurse I hear people say the house haunted and have ghosts," Janie teased and continued to stare at the ceiling.

Grace laughingly explained, "That's my new tenant well known to you all, Hakim Mansur."

"You mean he move across?" observed Victor politely.

"Ay ay, why?' came an exacting query from Janie.

Grace hesitated and searched the floor with lowered eyes.

"My tenant's reason I suppose is his business and I don't know that he wants to give his reason to anybody," said Grace with a matter-of-fact upright body posture.

"Do you think it has to do with the miserable lady next door?" Janie persisted.

"Amen Janie. I rent rooms. The man wanted a room and that's it. I was not going to question him why."

"He has such a long nose. Maybe he was poking it into her business and she chase him," Janie squealed, and she and Victor bent over in raucous laughter.

Grace moved to the edge of her seat and leaned forward with both hands on her knees, a hint to present company that their stay was overdue. The sound of footsteps and closing doors signaled the imminent appearance of Hakim, and Grace began to fidget with the cushions of the chairs in anticipation of Janie's prying interest.

"Ah! Hah! You could not want a better person for slave master," said an animated Victor and looked at Janie for approval.

"Yes of course, he has everything to make a real looking one," an enthusiastic Janie agreed. "And it not going to cost a penny."

"I don't want to be held responsible if anything happen to my guest because he is a stranger, and what they may do to him they will never do to you," a defensive Grace stood up signaling the meeting's end in the present venue.

Everyone finally left the room, Victor and Janie stood on the sidewalk and Grace in the doorway when they observed ex-convict Valdo making his way to his home in Baxter's Yard after a two-year absence spent in prison for robbery with violence.

Old fears crept back as they watched him approach the entrance to Baxter's Yard – the same busy walk of urgency with head held high in a posture to countenance all likely unwelcoming reactions. There were moments of hesitation when he made two attempts at lifting his arm before he could signal a greeting to the three outside Grace's house. Although well known to each other, neither party was at ease exchanging greetings.

There was a moment of distraction followed by a tense silence as Grace stepped aside to allow Hakim through the door. He mumbled something to her on his way out.

Victor and Jane were aching to know why the well-known tenant switched tenancy.

"This happen real fast right under our nose," Janie whispered to Victor as they moved a respectable distance from the departing guest to give an impression of noninterference.

"I didn't see any sign of this happening before, and now why she denying it," he confirmed, noting how the relationship had developed with stealthy overnight swiftness and now she reacting with evasive answers.

Just then, Valdo intruded and in an authoritative tone called out, "Mr. Mansur, a word with you please."

Hakim was halfway across the street when he stopped and turned around to face Valdo who was hurriedly approaching him with arm outstretched in anticipation of a handshake.

"Where does he know the man? Indiscreet!" Grace fretted to herself. "I so vex him just come from jail."

23

It was carnival Monday morning and the crowd had been up all night waiting, restless and eager to start on a predawn rhythmic explosion of frenetic reveling. The steel band out of Baxter's Yard practiced a few musical scales teasing a crowd all set to let loose onto the streets of Tabor City.

Some among those waiting were consuming alcoholic beverages in a bid to disable persisting inhibitions. Some arrived from predawn parties already shedding behavioral restraint, banging bottles and metal objects intent on unsettling the normal quietness of early morning.

The daybreak tradition referred to as "Ole Mas" was a slack expression of "old mask" represented by revelers dressed in costumes offering satirical depictions and lampooning persons and events currently in the news. It was a comic animation and amusing section of the festival.

Victor, Colom, Planche and Blackie were the best pan-men on Au Tabor and formed the "Sweet Melody Steel Orchestra," which had always attracted the largest following of merry makers among competing bands.

While revelers displayed gay abandon and merriment, the bandsmen maintained contrasting expressions of seriousness and importance applicable to professionals. They exhibited the conduct of captains and stewards responsible for the pleasurable trip and excessive fling of the motley crowd. The hyped expectation of this volatile crowd had to find energy from the syncopated rhythms of the steel band if it wanted to keep the number one ranking in crowd following because more pulsating music coming from another band could like a magnet pull a stream of revelers away.

"Da is crowd, Pardner," exhaled Colom who then called out to a short, thickset member of the band surrounded by six full size steel drums, "Papito, Papito, listen you know how you does fall asleep, don't play the fool. Make sure you don't drop the tempo."

"This band have more bass pan than any other band and I tell you already give me another bass player, all other band have four bass pan and is only this one band have six," Papito replied.

If Zoe didn't like to fight like that, I give him your place because he can cover all the beat better than you," Victor intervened.

"Now is not the time for this talk, aye fellas fifteen minutes to go, get ready."

The crowd surged forward with delirious shouts of approval as the throbbing bass and tenor pans of the steel band trounced the morning stillness. A two-day marathon of self-indulgent pleasure began in the city.

Invariably words to the music imported raunchy suggestions and were compositions by male calypso balladeers. The songs often offered a parody on how women dispense sexual favors in a one-sided mating storyline.

Over the next two days, the event was a surreal spectacle of boisterous revelers dancing on the streets in a costumed attempt to depict, with varying ineptitude, a bandleader's concocted fantasies. Many costumes were designed with minimal covering of the body, or conversely, to allow maximum permissible exposure using materials chosen with preference for brightness of colors enabling vivid impressions of the festival.

Participating in Tabor City carnival was a mix of all ages, classes and races. A montage of revelers that have overstepped all borders of decency in a resurgent comfort of their nakedness.

An important phase of the pageantry was a competition among the bands for the best costumes and depiction of themes. Selected winners were judged based on a complex system of multiple standards. Prizes awarded at a selected venue to winning bands were seldom received without contentious disagreement and debate. However the wild animation of the winners was cheered on by public address loudspeakers and radio broadcast as crowds of ecstatic dancers paraded in front the stage.

"This is real carnival spirit, an expression of freedom, a once a year cultural experience to jump and prance openly and unrestrained, nous pas mêlée, this is Au Tabor where we are happy," applauded the Emcee.

The Tuesday following was celebrated as the "last lap," and time was expiring for the one memorable rendering that would clearly depict this year's festival. So within the permitted time there was a passionate exertion by revelers to assimilate as much pleasurable feeling and experiences before the midnight hour and before commencement of the official forty-day tryst of fasting and abstinence on Ash Wednesday.

The limited time drove Grace, Janie and Chalky to dance and behave publicly in an intentionally lewd and shocking manner so the episode could withstand periodic recall in the interim prior to next year's carnival.

"Chalky feel like he is king, cutting style, woman on either side with arms around them," observed a normally aloof Tom Blyth as he watched Janie and Grace performing a sensual dance. Excitedly, he approached Grace and grabbed her around the waist attempting to pull her away from Chalky. Chalky reacted with protective hostility and struck Tom who retaliated with a sharp kick to Chalky's chest that knocked him to the ground.

Chalky was a diminutive replica of his father Ballast, but was determined to attain his father's invincibility by assuming a mantle of a gang leader. The steel band music faded jerkily and then ceased. The crowd scattered as band members turned combatants rushed to assist after learning of Chalky's downfall. Tom had a head start in a sprint away from the scene, and was chased by a group of Chalky's friends. Tom was a champion sprinter and arrived at the police station well ahead of his pursuers and went to the inner sanctuary of his father's office. A squad of police stood at the door to the police station facing a jeering crowd across the street.

With the pulse of carnival music still coursing through their heads, scores of the faithful sought a return to normalcy and participated in the rituals on Ash Wednesday.

24

Sometime before Victor's mother, Lorna, gave birth to her eighth child, he felt it incumbent as the eldest at the age of nineteen years to seek new lodgings. His father's recent decision to build an extension to accommodate the separation of gender among the siblings of four boys and three girls further influenced his resolve to make room for the expected addition to the family.

Victor was puzzled why owners of large houses had fewer children while those in cramped conditions had many children as evidenced in Baxter's Yard.

"Do all large families end up with smaller lodgings?"

Unsure whether the call was for temperance, he dismissed assertions by some of a disparity in intelligence and education as the reason for this pattern and stayed with his father's proclamation given its biblical adherence.

"God has blessed me with a wonderful treasure and I am keeping His wish to go forth and multiply."

These words supposedly of choice were often stated in defense of shortcomings when flustered over his inability to provide adequately for the needs of his family. He remembered, following a game of table tennis at the home of Vivian when he jokingly suggested staying in a spare apartment over the weekend. In return, he gave the assurance of a willingness to perform any chores around that Vivian might request of him.

Vivian immediately approved of the suggestion, "Great idea I will let my parents know, I am sure it will be alright with them."

Vivian's father was a surgeon at the island's main hospital and his mother owned a horticultural business. Both were reputed to be from wealthy families. Vivian, their only child, was able to assure him with such implicit confidence causing Victor to note how much Vivian was at liberty to determine his own circumstances. But he felt fortunate to be welcomed into spacious and comfortable living quarters.

There was no apparent diminution of pride although he had offered to perform some household chores. Vivian addressed only the issue of boarding and never mentioned a need for compensating duties.

Vivian and Victor developed a closer bond living in the same home and saluted each other with a V sign using the index and middle fingers to form the letter. The affability was enhanced through an academic appreciation for classical subjects, an aptitude not anticipated from a student of Victor's background. This provided further endorsement for Dr. and Mrs. Keswick to welcome Victor into that residence on a more permanent basis so joint study habits could progress and hopefully reflect in examination grades.

The vendetta between Zane Carter and the four buddies was no longer a hotbed issue. Zane was destined to enter the seminary and once the student body became cognizant of his vocational calling, he was treated with a passive response whenever he displayed his occasional tantrums. Concern over graduation and exams in the coming months greatly diminished the affiliation among the four students and was exacerbated by the rift between Victor and Tom, and the inevitable attachment of the two V's in residence. Issues and concerns belonging to the adult world began to widen the cracks in the ruptured bond.

"When I grow up I don't want to remain living here. After I graduate I will look for a good job overseas," mused Victor after learning a scholarship to Catholic University in Ireland had been approved to surprisingly, study medicine. His father Herman was overjoyed, having lobbied for the prestige of having a son with the title of "doctor." Catholic Church authorities welcomed this flagship opportunity hoping to counter an influx of Evangelical religions aggressively ministering among the underprivileged and were offering several theological study opportunities at Bible schools in their home country. The evangelical pastors were establishing more accessible and informal missions, which tolerated divergent and personalized interpretations of scripture by ordinary folk. The latest pastors had kept it basic and simple having instituted the bible as the central and sole required guidebook for salvation.

Thomas Blyth, captain of the school's Cadet Corps, had already secured admission to a military academy aided by the contacts of his father as local Police Commissioner. Vivian Keswick was guaranteed a place to study economics at his father's alma mater, Edinburgh University to which he was also a generous alumna.

In addition to the acceptance places of Tom Blyth, Vivian Keswick and Victor Provident already processed, the British council in a late response approved scholarships for studies in Law for Martin Innocent. Zane Carter was headed directly to the seminary in France. Martin Innocent said he was lovesick and planned to marry his girlfriend as soon as he graduated from school.

"I'm going to send for her as soon as I can while I'm up there," he disclosed this to Victor, who gave warning. "You been going steady for only four months. Man, you should wait a little longer until you all get to know each other better."

"Everybody telling me the same thing but I know for a fact we love each other and we discuss openly everything."

"Do your parents know of your plans?"

"What, you want my father to put me on one of his schooners and ship me out. But one thing I do not understand is why we not supposed to like girls when they are the sweetest thing on earth?"

25

The graduation of the first group of students from St. Teresa's College was a momentous occasion. The group had attained the highest level of educational instruction available on the island; a significant achievement for local youth. This qualified them to enter the workforce and perhaps begin training to work in any of the existing nonprofessional positions required on Au Tabor.

Victor was the only atypical student at the graduation ceremony. In effect, he stood out as a resident of Baxter's Yard at variance with the parade of young men from socially prominent parentage and who could afford the school fees. He was dressed in his best clothes and looked plain next to fellow students in tailored suits. His long-sleeved shirt was puffed at the waist of his tightly belted khaki twill trousers with broad shoulders defining his athletic build.

Miss Mable, accompanied by Victor's parents Mr. and Mrs. Provident, were on hand to add to particulars surrounding the achievements of the youngster from Baxter's Yard. Miss Mable also felt graduated from a solitary existence and saw this as a step up to activity outside of the church doors.

Interaction between sponsor and Provident family during the graduation ceremony was constrained and revealed the upper limit of the relationship. Miss Mable never hankered after gratitude and only wanted to be elevated to the status of charitable person. Victor had not been able to feel a sense of appreciation for the Mable Baxter scholarship even though his parents often spoke with anxiety of the consequences if her financial support was withdrawn. He felt uneasy whenever their paths crossed, recalling as a young boy how she always patted him on the back with a cautionary saying, "Hope you are being a good boy," but never seemed to be interested in a personal chat. When he grew past adolescence and developed into a robust, athletic young man, an awkward period ensued. The a middle-aged spinster became apprehensive of young men who may have been influenced by standards of morality and aggression peculiar to Baxter's Yard.

On the assembly hall stage stood Bishop Goodrich who presided over the graduation as the main celebrant with headmaster Father O'Connor and other faculty clerics performing formalities of certificate distribution, prize giving and self congratulatory speeches outlining achievements of the past year. A highlight of the evening was an appeal by the bishop to attend more to the needs of the underprivileged. He noted the outstanding achievement of Victor and in so doing praised the role Miss Mable played as exemplifying a Christian way of life.

Beneath an eighteenth-century style bonnet and matching black ankle length dress with neckline collar and long sleeves, Miss Mable conversed with graceful ease among the white-robed clerics. Finally the bishop parted the gathered clerics and met with Miss Mable who clasped her hands devoutly, curtsied to kiss his ring with embellished humility.

"Your Grace, you knew I would feel self-conscious when you congratulated me for helping Victor but it came naturally once I saw the need."

"You have never failed to demonstrate your concern for your community and in particular the underprivileged and for this you deserve all the accolades bestowed," countered the bishop.

"Your Grace, I have a request which I hope you will grant me," implored Miss Mable.

"Certainly, what is it?" replied the bishop with assurance.

"Remember I told you during my visit to Lourdes I purchased a large statue of Our Lady? Well, I organized a miniature tabernacle for her in a corner of my living room. I am hoping you will accept my invitation to personally bless and sanctify the room."

"My powers of consecration are no higher than that of your parish priest, and I am further restricted by the train of liturgical and ceremonial assistants required."

"Oh, I understand and maybe should have known better," admitted Miss Mable and accepted an alternate offer from the bishop who advised:

"Why not allow the shrine to be placed in an appropriate place in the sanctuary of the church where it will receive consecration during regular mass?"

26

Au Tabor was about to be divested of its youthful vigor. The vitality, academic and athletic abilities embodied in the five students was a national asset unrealized before and had suddenly grown in worth. These young men were about to embark on a journey aboard the large passenger ship, S.S. Andalucía alongside the wharf for study in the United Kingdom. While an anticipated ten-year absence for professional qualification was laudable, the loss of talent evoked a shout of mock despair.

"What are we to do without our best opening-batsmen, pace-bowler, and center-forward?" Half-hearted cheers greeted the outburst.

The night gave rise to a poignant scene marking the commencement of a new chapter. The folks who had gathered to say farewell were overwrought with pride and promise of fresh goals yet anxious about the future. In the background, the towering hull of the steamer S.S. Andalucía, with a multiethnic crew, was about to take five precious young citizens far away to England.

The night was also eventful for island people from all sections of Au Tabor they came together on the apron of the wharf to say bon voyage. Notably, the largest group present was made up of the proud residents of Baxter's Yard who had come to say farewell to Victor.

The nervous giggles were brief and departing was accepted as a worthy sacrifice to the teary-eyed groups of well-wishers gathered in pockets of family, girlfriends and close pals of the five students. Diligently, the departing students made the rounds, consoling everyone with a vague promise to stay in touch.

Their girlfriends never complained or asked why they had to remain at home, why only the boys had been given the opportunity to travel overseas for study. They were in the tradition of their mothers, ladies in waiting for a marriage proposal.

Lorna's maternal heartache cried out publicly for her departing son, "God only knows when I will see my eldest child again," she moaned.

"Don't worry, I'll be back, I'll be back," Victor consoled.

"Don't go fighting any war and join anybody army, okay?" Lorna sniffled back.

Mr. Provident disagreed with the advice and wanted bragging rights for his son. "You can't decide for the boy, Lorna. It is a different kind of life in a big country. Suppose the boy doing so well and they believe in him?"

"That can't be the glow from the setting sun," an alert person in the crowd remarked aloud, "Hey, that looks like a fire!" someone else shouted.

"A fire yes, over there!" another individual was pointing to an orange glow in the distance above the rooftops.

"It looks like a house right in town. I wonder whose home it is." This expressed concern was followed by a loud murmur and a peeling away of persons from the gathering on the docks. Those who remained became more nervous and uneasy when Police Commissioner Blyth, Tom's father left at full trot after being summoned by a policeman.

Passengers were scheduled to board within an hour for departure two hours after but everything turned into chaos.

27

It was not long before Tabor City began showing signs of alarm and turmoil in dismay of a menacing looking fire around suppertime. Every household was alerted, bringing occupants to a standstill in doorways, on front steps and sidewalks while staring anxiously at the inferno. The evening's gusting winds fanned the flames into a lashing and curling fury that churned the stomachs of onlookers.

Some men were hurrying down a street ahead of the fire shouting something to residents. From a distance, they seemed to alarm persons causing them to clasp their heads in their hands; some raised both arms sending distress signals when first they understood what was being said. "No water, no water in the fire hydrant. The fire engine cannot find water to put out the fire."

On hearing the shouts, Mr. Blanchet stepped out of a nearby post office carrying a bundle of files and stared at the men shouting alarmingly.

"Who gave you authority to spread this false rumor? I will have you arrested for causing panic!"

"Shut your stupid ugly face! You goin' arrest me because they have no water?" jeered one of the men.

"You ugly fool, they have water to hose the bucket shit off the street every morning but don't have to out the fire," observed another and suggested a relevant designation. "This is a "Shit Brigade' not a 'Fire Brigade.'"

"Go arrest the fire instead that coming for your backside."

The severity and brutal shock of the information devastated residents of Tabor City. Pouring water on a fire was the only known course of action by which it could be extinguished. Nothing in their past or imagined future would have signaled the destruction of their livelihood by an out-of-control conflagration unchallenged by a helpless fire brigade without a water supply. Entire families were moving in a constant stream along the streets away from the fire carting on their heads, backs and arms bundles of their clothes and household belongings.

Meanwhile fire had engulfed five houses on the same side of the street and two across the street. Aided by strong winds, it was evident the fire was spreading in all directions and was now a raging inferno, exhaling roaring sounds amid the loud clatter of collapsing structures.

All who came to say goodbye had left the docks ahead of departure time. The students were hastily urged to board the steamer to allow well-wishers an opportunity to turn attention to this potentially dangerous fire.

Vivian, Tom and Martin complied without delay, but Victor and Zane looked apprehensively in the direction of the fire. The suburban residences of the three who boarded were absolutely safe unlike the threat to homes and communities occupied by the families of Victor and Zane.

Evacuation of homes in the city was no longer a matter for deliberation and all city residents began the process, except Miss Mable whose unruffled reaction had a dithering effect on the start of evacuation activity in Baxter's Yard. This community accustomed to her issuing the go-ahead signal of proceedings monitored her standing in the balcony staring in the direction of the fire, stoically viewing a fiery Thespian landscape. Her tenants were dreading the approaching destructive force desperately conceding powers to her in a desperate gamble she would be able to prevent the conflagration from reaching Baxter's Yard.

The fire continued to leap from house to house four blocks away from Baxter's Yard and showed no sign of abating. Moreover, it was also spreading in all directions while surging primarily in a forward motion. Apparently this may have begun a waning in confidence of the Baxter sisters. Diana Baxter brought onto the middle of the street a small table followed closely by sister Mable with the three-foot statue of Our Lady whom she stood on the table facing the fire flanked by holy pictures and other religious icons. That was the only time Our Lady was moved from her house crèche since consecration some months before.

The tenants of Baxter's Yard saw this as a loss of confidence and began hurriedly moving out with their meager belongings. They considered this action by the sisters as ceding all hope to iconic props used regularly by everyone with a poor record of evident success.

At that point, the city was sitting under a glowing red bowl that had suffused the night sky, helpless in the path of marching flames forcing desperate residents to resort to extreme action of tossing bulky and unwieldy valuables from second story balconies and windows onto the streets below hoping they would somehow be conveyed to safety. Sparks crackled, vaulted and danced furiously ahead of the flames falling uncomfortably close to evacuees engaged in last minute salvaging efforts.

Victor gave no indication of making plans to board the steamer.

This night of catastrophic scenes and specter of Armageddon had Victor uncertain that his mind could be trusted. He pondered if it was an omen, the precise timing of his imminent departure, how was he to interpret this confluence of events? Irrespective of boarding time, Victor was determined to await the first flame that would dare to lick the wooden frame of the Provident family shelter.

While every family member attempted to carry the maximum belongings, an unprecedented number of decisions and options were perhaps frantically being considered.

What things should I take with me to go? How am I going to carry all the things I want to take? Where can I go tonight if my home is destroyed in the fire?

The Provident family — father and mother, and eight offspring stood silently next to salvaged possessions. The ill-fated moment drew near with the fire igniting the neighboring hut. The horn of the steamer scheduled to depart soon gave a loud groan with an accompanying shriek as in a great effort to be heard above the commotion. At that moment the town was facing disaster and every manner of sound or clamor was perceived in distress. All protective and defensive procedures were failing before the raging inferno. The whistle of the steamer sounded again in a further call for passengers to board for departure. Herman and Lorna and their three eldest children turned sharply to look at Victor, disregarding the fire momentarily. He angled his gaze above their heads and could hear his mother's faint sobs. No words were spoken. Victor stood his ground until the flames rushed onto the roof of the family hut.

"Let us go!" shouted Victor in an emotional but authoritative voice. Picking up their allotted bundles, they hurried out of the Yard onto the street no longer able to endure the extreme heat.

There was bedlam on the streets of Tabor City a scene of swarming displaced residents, some pausing briefly to rest as they struggled with the contents of their households. The incessant beeping of a car horn by David Baxter added to the panic-stricken environs as he sought to alert his sisters to the threat of being trapped. The fire was already threatening their block a couple doors away with half the city already ruined by the fire. David sped from his suburban home to the city and on arrival made his sisters abandon their vain attempt at holding up the fire through divine intervention. Although assured of comfortable lodgings in their brother's mansion, they were in a state of shock, unable to countenance the loss of the home, an heirloom and architectural treasure. The main bereavement surrounded the armoire before which they stood praying solemnly hoping for a miracle. The armoire was cabinet furniture of the finest joinery. Standing over six feet in height with meticulously designed double doors overlaid with full length mirrors, it was located in the main bedroom and held a prized selection of valuables acquired over a lifetime by Miss Mable. The collection comprised a wide-ranging assortment of household linens and furnishings, lingerie, crockery, cutlery and jewelry.

Their brother scolded them for delaying and not securing more items from the house as his sisters made their final exit with suitcases of clothing adequate for a holiday weekend. The Provident clan, all nine, stood next to the steps of the Baxter front door amongst their bundled possessions secured in bed sheets, boxes and crates except for Victor's travel packed new suitcase. They lingered unclear in purpose, without a plan and could not offer an explanation for their presence. Everyone stood silently.

"An alien force is attacking and we are unable to see and identify them. We are without a defense and unable to retaliate," offered David, his purpose for being scornfully absurd was to confound their minds and undermine any possible request for assistance knowing his sister had been a past sponsor.

"What are you doing here? I thought you were supposed to be on the ship," blurted Miss Mable addressing Vivian without breaking off her stride to the car.

As the fire raged unabated the authorities eventually realized they were dealing with an out of control existential beast. The water supply that could have doused the fire into submission and perhaps brought it under control was unavailable and so a determination was made to take away from its ignitable path the fuel it would need to carry on its march of fiery demolition, in other words starve the beast. And so began the battle of resolve with ammunition of dynamite employed in the destruction of unaffected buildings thought to be in the enabling path of an iniquitous fire.

In the hours just before dawn the combatants appeared exhausted. The signal smoke of dying embers hovered low over the desolate scene. Tenuous claims of success in the night's battle pointed to important buildings saved; among them were the imposing Catholic Cathedral and surrounding primary schools and the college and convent secondary schools. However although the physical structures stood, the institutions were now without the attending congregations and student bodies presently dispersed all around the island.

28

Tabor City overnight had transformed into a huge crematory in which lay the city's ashes and skeletal remains. The funeral pyre of former residential and commercial buildings was a charred dust and a morning drizzle made a grimy paste on its concrete bones, which only a few hours before supported urban life. Metal bedsprings coiled out of shape among the charred ruins were excruciating reminders to many who slept comfortably on previous nights and were now in search of a resting place. There were no warnings or impending signs, no last gasp. The fire hounded the populace out of the city arbitrarily, vulgarly and mercilessly. Perhaps an allegory of life was symbolized by each wisp of smoke curling upwards into ghostlike shapes out of the blackened surface.

The outskirts of the city was spotted with camp style settlements under trees, in parks, in derelict structures and empty school buildings while overcrowded homes of families and friends did their best to cope with the overload. There was an exodus to north and south Au Tabor upsetting the established demography for political representation. At first the hotels are accepting requests for accommodation by persons displaced and who could afford to pay but after being roundly criticized for lacking in compassion special rates were offered for those whose homes were destroyed in the blaze.

While Tabor City was ablaze, Nurse Grace intercepted every able-bodied man and woman on his or her way out of the Yard with their skimpy belongings. She handed each a portable item or items of furniture linen and wares, contents of the house with instructions to deposit them on the grounds adjacent to the nurse's quarters of the hospital.

It was the most complete rescue operation given the available manual resource of Baxter's Yard and also due recompense for the nurse and midwife who nurtured and cared the sick and injured of Baxter's Yard.

Nurse Grace captivated parents with stories about their children from birth, those who caused prolonged labor and those who hardly cried and cried loudest claiming to know the innate personality of each newborn. In a delicate caper of combining hereditary material with normal expected behavior, she predicted lofty professional achievements for the youth of Baxter's Yard and boasted how she unofficially adopted them as her family.

"All dem so is my family," she said, making a sweeping gesture with her arm to incorporate all the individuals lounging among the furniture spread about the grounds of the nurse's hostel. However the night watchman saw the situation as a potential embarrassment and expressed his concern,

"Nurse, tell me how we gonna get rid of these people especially now they have no place to go?" inquired the night watchman. "When Matron come and see dat she goin blow a fuse, family or no family."

29

Former residents of burnt out Tabor City were on the move, dispersing to unfamiliar parts of Au Tabor, stranded and uncertain of the next step, which at this juncture seemed hopeless. Victor and his family drifted on the outskirts of Tabor City throughout the night in the company of some other fire displaced crowds. Sleepless and traumatized, they were without a known destination and purpose except to await the arrival of sunrise.

Streaks of crimson appeared among grey clouds over the eastern sky heralding a rising sun. The morning scene unleashed new pain and malady of spirit among the homeless victims when at this precise hour prior to this wretched morning, a window opened welcoming the morning light and letting in fresh breezes with the hum of familiar morning sounds. In another room the mumbling voices of waking children, and the clatter of dishes and cutlery all in preparation for the day's work, school or play. They are now indefinitely deprived of domestic function performed in familiar quarters.

The scale of such a disaster on minds unprepared and in denial kept the displaced searching for clues around them to reinforce knowledge that they were awake. The senses were impaired and unable to resolve events of the past twelve hours and seek meaning and reasons in the imponderables of a three letter word thrice repeated, "why, why, why?"

"You know we will never understand how God works," exclaimed Herman Provident while observing the despair on faces of fire victims lining the roadside among their salvaged possessions.

"Where we going, who going help us?" cried Ma Reggie revealing her distress over an unimaginable state of helplessness.

The women ignored Herman's pronouncement in search for more concrete solutions

"Yes Lord, what we gonna do?" Lorna joined in search of a practical assistance.

"I hear Nurse Grace and my friends are up the road at the nurse's quarters. Maybe we should join them?" Victor suggested.

Herman did not welcome the suggestion and blasted Victor. "Boy, even at this time you are only thinking of going to meet women, especially when you should have been on your way to study. What help are you now that you stayed behind? Ma Baxter was right, you should have been on the boat to England."

"Leave the boy alone," Lorna cautioned and then became concerned when Victor grabbed his packed suitcase and was walking quickly away.

"Victor, where you going? Come back here. It's okay Victor, come back," she pleaded, taking some steps toward Victor before he broke into a determined trot up the road.

"You know, if you had just tell the boy to go on the boat it would be alright, he would have gone. Now you want to persecute him," Lorna said, eying her husband.

"The boy is not a baby. Look all the others board the ship, so why couldn't he follow them? And furthermore, I was busy saving things from the fire."

Ma Reggie a former Baxter's Yard resident saw a complex explanation for any new occurrence. "You see because of wha happen last night, confusion going start, is like if the world ending and everybody going to blame everybody for everything."

30

All constabulary and associated law enforcement personnel were called out on duty and reserves from Northern and Southern Au Tabor districts were ordered to fill in for the many police of Tabor City affected by the fire. Members of an army battalion from a neighboring island were also arriving to provide support.

Victor sought friendly community to assuage his being unjustly rebuked. It would be difficult to contain his anguish and regain emotional calm without the company of Nurse Grace and other friends from Baxter's Yard. Additionally, his scholarly mind anticipated a deficiency due to the departure of his fellow students the previous evening.

However, he had to undertake an important mission before joining the others at the nurse's quarters. For the preceding six months, he had been a lodger in the helper's quarters at the home of Vivian's parents and was on his way to try to get back this favorable concession. The current chaos made Victor doubtful the Keswick family knew he had not sailed with the other students and while on his way to their residence he rehearsed his explanation for not departing as expected. His exchanges with the Keswick elders were minimal, as Vivian would liaise in most situations on his behalf.

Some twenty minutes from the Keswick residence, he heard gunshots nearby and then suddenly a few young men appeared running at full speed carrying various unwrapped goods with a couple of armed police in pursuit. Victor was walking in the same direction as the men ran and in self-preservation rushed into a recess to the side of a house.

"Put your hands up!" ordered a policeman pointing his rifle at Victor who raised one hand holding on to the suitcase with the other.

"Drop the suitcase and put both hands up!"

Victor complied and shouted nervously, "I can explain, I can explain!"

The policeman ignored his offer and called on another police. "Come, I got one cornered here."

"I can explain everything!" Victor insisted, realizing the accents were of migrants employed as auxiliary security by the tourism industry in Southern Au Tabor. The other policemen were returning without any captured suspects and none of them seemed to be natives of Au Tabor. The police paid scant attention to a handcuffed Victor and instead gathered around his suitcase making various comments after opening it up.

"He sure got a lot to explain."

"Yeah, man nearly everything in there brand new."

"He must have spent the whole time packing, see how everything neat and well folded."

Finally a police with sergeant stripes addressed Victor with a two-pronged question. "Where do you live? Do you have a job?"

"I am a student just graduated and I was on my way to England to further my studies." The sergeant sighed and shook his head suggesting Victor had given a bogus answer that was considered so implausible it prompted another policeman to put a finger to his temple indicating Victor could be mentally unstable.

"Does this road take you to England," asked another attempting humor by way of ridicule.

"Do you live around here?" the sergeant continued.

"No our house got burnt in the fire last night."

"Then what are you doing around here and where did you steal this suitcase of clothes and toilet articles?"

An enraged Victor startled the group with a voice blast gesturing passionately with his hands.

"It belongs to me and I did not steal it. All of you can go to hell." Victor focused his rage on the accusation of theft without further explanation. He knew facing a group of single-minded skeptics he would not be believed and was resolute in avoiding the second part of the question. The sergeant had hoped to extract some new leads, but Victor dreaded any mention of the Keswick family knowing it would result in an unsavory involvement for them and intrude uncomfortably on his connections with the family. Irrespective of his innocence, the insinuation that residents of Baxter's Yard were always having disputes with the law had received further substantiation.

This neighborhood was similar to the Keswick's; the houses were surrounded by well-groomed lawns and exquisite flower gardens with jalousie gable windows ensuring the desire of the wealthy for secrecy and privacy. Except for the occasional high-pitched bark of tiny dogs, the quiet and staid surroundings suggested the houses were devoid of occupants but Victor was sure liveried eyes, wealthy maidens and alcoholic wives were peering at him causing frissons of shame to clamber all over his body.

"How old are you?

"Nineteen."

"You know where to find your mother or your father."

"Of course, I am not a bastard like you and your gang."

A police club struck the back of Victor's leg forcing his collapse on to his knees. This was followed by a gun butting to his back that sent him further forward onto his hands. Victor remained on hands and knees surrounded by police boots. He listened to their strange accents that promoted thoughts in him of some undetected power having control of his destiny and was using nefarious means to hamper his future prospects. In a courageous embrace of spirit, he staked his innocence against this injustice while recalling tales of an innocent Jesus Christ crucified by the soldiers while the government stood by. He conversed silently with the influential voices of Father Limos and Miss Mable who vouched for his innocence. Comforted in thought, he meditated with closed eyes to intensify visions of last night's fiery scenes as a companion to his physical pain and mental anguish.

Passing vehicles slowed down and occupants gazed unhappily at Victor, pedestrians paused with sealed lips, without query or comment. The enforcers of law and order trained to control and subjugate were parading Victor as the prize, with suitcase evidence, bogus travel excuse after being apprehended in the vicinity of an exclusive neighborhood. There was no reprieve in the public's mind for such measures were necessary to curb unlawful activity. Victor was the new pariah, born and raised in Baxter's Yard.

31

The four students on board the steamer S.S. Andalucía spent many hours listening to the world news, in particular the British Broadcasting Corporation. It was two days since they sailed out of Au Tabor, a British colony, and so news on the BBC was the favored source.

World broadcasts portrayed Tabor City as totally burnt down and urgently in need of all forms of aid because its devastated people had lost all their possessions. Tents, blankets, clothing and food supplies were among the immediate requirements. The students were consoled by news that many countries were mobilizing to have those items sent without delay.

"I feel like a deserter," said Tom as they huddled in common concern. "My island is under siege by some arsonist while we are relaxing in this comfortable lounge."

"Stop your military talk. You ain't even reach England yet," Martin cautioned.

"You can only be considered a deserter when you abscond from your duty. I see no parallel in your intentions prior to the fire," summed up Vivian.

"And they have no arson. It started in a tailor shop only two blocks from our house. A good thing it was downwind from us," Zane clarified.

"So how does this prove it's not arson?"

"My parents know the tailor well and believe he may have left a hot iron on some clothes."

"Instead of feeling sorry for persons who lost everything in the fire, you are offering silly excuses for a family friend ahead of any proper investigation."

"We should be using this anticipated seclusion to empathize with the fire victims in their distress. Unhelpful recrimination will not turn this ship around so we can be with them," Vivian lectured.

"You know who people going to praise because he stayed behind with his family? Victor Provident, of course," Tom continued in his resentful tone.

"How you know he's not regretting staying behind?" challenged Zane.

"No way, because he made it as a poor boy he believes he is some star."

"Victor is an unassuming soul, disinclined to promoting himself," Vivian spoke firmly sensing attempts to malign Victor.

"That's what you think? Why stay behind? What can he do to help?"

"What the man do you? You on the man back, everything he do you have to criticize," Zane confronted Tom.

Martin and Vivian let out grunts of approval. "Yeah, un huh!"

Tom glanced around at the faces of his three companions and chose not to respond, quietly bowing his head and grumbled, "Eight more days of cabin confinement before arriving at port."

32

Au Tabor Island was a garrison during and before the 1914-1918 war because of its unique topography of sheltered harbors and lookout promontories. To complete this facility as a military station for many campaigns from the days of Tudor, a complex to provide housing for living quarters and warehouses was constructed on the site.

The construction of sturdy brick and stone barracks had withstood the wear of time and though unoccupied for several decades, they were still habitable and brought immense relief to several displaced families irrespective of their prior situation. For many bourgeois families, maintaining their former elitist front proved to be untenable. They were now rubbing shoulders with the likes of the Provident family who had secured a two-room facility in one of the barracks, which had a large communal kitchen with an antiquated wood-burning stove.

Lorna was preparing the first lunch following the fire while chatting and becoming acquainted with other ladies living in the building. She was relating some recent affairs of her family to a lady next door whom she sought to befriend.

"Even though what happen between my son and his father, I am cooking extra for my son because as I told you when he was to leave for England he said I will be back three times," she paused to obtain something from another section of the kitchen and continued on her return,

"But that was when he was going away to England. He means that all the time, he is a loving boy but very sensitive and hurts easily," explained Lorna. "Sometimes I am not so sorry he did not catch the boat."

Suddenly Herman burst into the kitchen and Lorna was about to greet him when she noticed his face looked disturbed and his body trembled as he related the message.

"Oh my God, they arrest Victor. The police arrest Victor!"

Lorna started wailing and seemed to be losing balance, but Herman quickly hugged her as a precaution. Her screams were loud enough to set off an alarm among displaced occupants already irritable and distressed. They dropped their chores and streamed toward the kitchen.

"What he do? Why they holding him, my first boy?"

Chalky and a couple friends arrived in the kitchen and updated the gathering, "They say he teef clothes he was carrying in a grip."

The heat of a midday sun sent temperature soaring and while it did not possess the devastation of last night's combustive heat, it brought to near boiling point agitated former Baxter's Yard residents protesting Victor's arrest. A curfew had been imposed on movement in an area of the city to curb looting of abandoned shops and buildings scorched but not totally burnt. The police compound across the river was never threatened. Recruited security and non-Tabor militia confronted the horde marching in defiance of the curfew. They reacted predictably in the maintenance of law and order, deploying men with protective shields, baton and an armed contingent bringing up the rear.

Herman stood at the entry to the bridge frantically waving to discourage the advancing protesters on their way to Police Headquarters. The exit to the bridge was heavily guarded by riot-clad police.

Herman, always a seeker of compromise was well received by upper classes as a pacifier of inflamed tensions. He had worked for many of that set and had their respect for his quality of work and trustworthiness.

"Look here and listen to me," Herman exhorted the crowd. "I am going to speak to some people who will help me," and reassured, "I know a lot of important people that can get them to release Victor."

"Mate always defending those people," came a shout from the crowd and others continued.

"They must be paying him!"

"What happen to mate? Messieurs our place burn down and we have no place to sleep."

"I thought you all were marching to free Victor," Herman reminded the protesters.

"Yeah, but why you stopping us?"

"No, no I just showing you an easier way."

A protester emerged from the crowd and stood before Herman. "Is that same easy way they using to arrest Victor and all of us, because the man have his new clothes." Another emerged in a face-to-face confrontation with Herman. "I bet if it was the fella who gone away am…. Vivian, Dr. Keswick son or the police chief son especially who had a suitcase of clothes, they would not arrest him."

Herman decided to issue a caution. "It don't matter what you know or think. You see how they waiting for you on the other side of the bridge to maul your backsides."

Meanwhile Victor stared at the prison cell walls, at the layers of paint peeling and bruised by graffiti curses and obscenities that were explicit dissenting expressions of previous occupants. The cubicle was furnished with only a child-sized fiber mattress and was cynically referred to as a "holding cell."

The guards were chatting and laughing, unconcerned they could be heard by the prisoner, "Where does Percival Harris alias Valdo hang out since the fire?" a police voice inquired.

"Sir, you mean that thief living in Baxter's Yard? You know I does see him moving with Hakim very often," a lower ranking voice informed,

"Hakim, Hakim?" The voice quizzed.

"The white fella with a big nose selling clothes from a suitcase in the villages."

"Oh, Mr. Mansur, he better watch this guy Valdo. He will fleece him in no time."

"Chief, why don't you warn Hakim about this guy?"

"Don't you worry I will soon bring him in for that robbery of two nights ago."

A third voice with a ring of alarm chimed in, "Boss, is Hakim who giving him the alibi that he was with him at the time of the robbery."

"Never mind, I will have a chat with Mr. Mansur."

The police conversation Victor just overheard caused pangs of fear and anger to intermingle in his stomach and heightened concern for his favorite brother, twelve year-old Johnny, a bright, carefree and adventurous youngster. From the general picture of conversation by the policemen at the front desk, Victor feared the trap had already been laid for his younger brother. After reviewing in his mind how many young males within Baxter's Yard were being carted off to prison and locked up, Victor considered how improbable it was to erase the stigma of prison, crime and anti social behavior on the reputation of Baxter's Yard. Herman Provident prided his household as one of the few that had never been subjected to a police investigation.

"My house is without stain, and we must defend it against all kinds of attack" was a typical homily he expressed to his family and such concern confirmed the vulnerability of those families in Baxter's Yard. Herman was often instilled with a variety of precepts when employers are pleased with his work.

This weighed heavily on Victor's mind and shifted the spotlight on those predisposed to become prisoners, like hero prisoners who had fought in defense of their country and were captured and imprisoned. So he anxiously likened himself to a captive of the aftermath of a confusing mystery of events followed by the expected questions, what were the alleged grounds for him being detained?

He recalled the bond of friendship between his school friends when they stood up and protected each other and mulled over the probable reaction if this misunderstanding had occurred to Vivian or Tom. Their parents must have been informed of his arrest and wondered why he has not had a visit from them. Gloom, hurt and beginning spasms from hunger dimmed his mental faculty and confidence. He regretted his decision to walk away from his family, which made him question his ability to make a go on his own. He had never missed the absence of his family as he did at that moment.

33

Herman hurried back to his two-room hostel in the old-fashioned brick walled barracks that served his family as a transit station. Only required essentials were removed from bundles of personal items lying on the floor while the younger children were playfully chasing in between the spaces.

His wife Lorna met him at the door. Her face carried the strains and streaks of deep anxiety, "How is he? Did you all speak, what he said?"

"Not yet. They had a set of them causing the police to block road to the station."

"But why the police blocking the road?"

"It's like I told them they making things worse saying they going to protest Victor's arrest."

"So when will we be able to see him?" A tone of heartache in Lorna's voice was evident as she covered her face with both hands to remove her present view of disappointing events and turn her thoughts inwards.

"Just wait I will show them, I work already for Miss Mable brother's wife's brother, well he is the Attorney General, Miss Mable had send me to do a job for him." Herman attempted to console Lorna with his self-important connections as a solution but she was skeptical, "So you think he will remember you?"

"Let me tell you when you do good work for somebody they will always remember you. Get the children ready, we all going by Miss Mable and I will leave it to her to arrange everything."

"It far from here, so how we getting there?"

Herman did not reply but left in a hurry with the impression he was going to fix the transport problem.

Migrant dwellers on the steep eastern slopes overlooking Tabor City were watching the daylight scene of a city mutilated by the blazing marauder the night before. They walked around listlessly and in despair. No more trekking down narrow muddy tracks to do the city's daily menial jobs that helped alleviate their poverty. They were among the latest settlers from north Au Tabor and Plasscan Valley squatting on the hillside's steep contours between dry gullies in crude shelters built from remnant material.

Nearby boxes with soil sprouting leafy greens, herbs and seasonings are splashed with remaining household water. Claims to fruit bearing trees on the borders of arbitrarily fenced off plots failed to resolve the ownership of fruit laden branches spreading into adjoining backyards and was a source of frequent contention.

Rowdy and hostile behavior relegated them to the darkest interpretations of a peasant class. They possessed an uncanny ability to create slum settlements that overwhelm neighborhoods with the stealth of a giant amoeba. Those squatters in particular erected their shacks with very little space in between, often restricted to the width of a door or window opening. Irregular formation and random positioning made it difficult to identify individual units enabling the variegated collection of hovel to expand imperceptibly in any direction.

Lorna hailed from a family of the earliest migrants of the hill. She looked out the window to watch Herman go in search of his friend and shrugged her shoulders in frustration over the contradictions besetting her husband, a poor man desperately wanting to wear a rich man's halo. In her opinion, those of her background should face the challenges head on. She presumed evidently rich people were gifted with a special luck which poor people were unable to access. In accord with her perceived disadvantaged position, she advocated people of her status should always be struggling to maintain an aggressive posture to counter the natural luck and influence of rich people if there was to be a just situation.

A truck unloading emergency supplies at the hostel stirred thoughts of the inconveniences she had encountered from living two miles outside the burnt city. Before the fire, Lorna was used to a stroll around the corner or walked a few blocks to obtain services and supplies or to pursue social activity. Her mind raced through plans of a chance to visit Victor at the Police station, which the unloaded truck presented. With the prospect of quick transportation into the city before Herman returned. Lorna raced down a flight of stairs to the truck parked next to the landing.

"Will you be going back to the city when you finish?" Lorna smiled alluringly at the driver of the truck.

He unfolded his arms and in mock disclosure said, "Lady, they have no more city left. Tell me where you want to go and I will drop you there."

"Can you bring me to, to, or better yet if you passing by the church I will stop there?" She spoke indecisively.

"Church? Is church you going to? You don't sound so sure," observed the driver. But then told her, "well hurry up I'll wait for you.

34

Lorna dashed inside, dressed, instructed her eldest daughter Sophie to look after the children, rushed into the kitchen, made up a lunch parcel and rejoined the driver. Lorna sat next to the driver who directed his helper to ride in the cargo tray.

"Is who you bringing food for? Not the priest, I hope."

"Why you want to know people business like that?"

"Is because the food smelling good I want to know who going to enjoy it."

"Well, is not you, so mind your business."

"Why you behaving so now, you were so nice at first."

"Oh so you can tell me what you want and I must just take it," Lorna wanted to keep the upper hand and continued. "Is so you men does think women is a doormat."

"Wait miss, I ain't understand how you reach there."

"Well, I not waiting for you to disrespect me 'cause you done tell me I bringing food for priest."

The driver managed a statement of joint regret and defense.

"It's my habit to make joke but I didn't know you were thin skin."

Lorna reacted to a sudden increase in speed of the truck. "If you driving crazy put me down because I have a husband and eight children to take care of and to be responsible for."

Lorna had been anxious to get this message out, hoping it would communicate or explain her reaction and inform him of her circumstances. It should say to him she was thankful and was not displaying ingratitude but she had to make it abundantly clear that she accepted the ride as an upright and respectable family person on her way to church.

The truck stopped in front the church and Lorna got off offering her thanks that went unanswered. The driver ignored her completely and did not drive off immediately but reached for a pack of cigarettes and proceeded to light one.

Lorna was only a short walk away from the police station but was aware the truck had not driven off immediately. To guard against being shamed as a liar she walked into church hoping the truck driver would leave after she disappeared beyond the doors. The candlelit setting of inside the church struck a sudden discordant note in Lorna. It brought to the fore a sense of right and wrong for her deceitful use of a holy place. The thought soon brought her to her knees in prayer and view this experience as an omen directing her to pray for Victor's release from police custody.

After fifteen minutes of prayer and uncertainty about whether the truck driver was still lurking outside, Lorna decided to leave church through the side door of the belfry area accessed mainly by clerics and church functionaries.

Entering the church at the same time was Father Limos almost colliding with Lorna at the door and calmly greeting her.

"Mrs. Provident you have been uppermost in my thoughts since I learnt of Victor's problems."

She had to compose herself before she began an apology. "Father this thing make me shame so much that is why I passing by this door."

"Oh, never mind through whatever door you enter God's Temple, you will be welcome."

"I going to see him now and bring some food for him."

"It is good you have decided to put Victor's problem in God's hands."

"Father, he have no problem, everyone know is not his fault why they holding him inside there," Lorna expressed firmly. "At least you can speak to him and tell him everything will be alright if you feel so."

"I'm sorry, I am due to conduct a funeral service in the next half hour. But give him this." Father Limos opened his large missal and handed Lorna a leaflet with the title Psalm 26: "When he reads this it will give him strength courage to overcome all evil."

Lorna could not hide her disappointment and didn't try. "All that well and good, Father, but it not giving him his freedom."

35

Herman nabbed Jacko out of the arms of his prized concubine, Sissy. An exchange of favors was always anticipated between Herman, the helpful handyman and Jacko, owner of a truck for hire. Sissy complained. "So just so you come and take my man away from me?"

Jacko did little to resist an arm pull by Herman while he savored the complaint. It was a source of manly pride to hear possessive comments from her.

"You see what you doing to my lady. Man I can't find another like her."

"I'll make sure I bring him straight back for you," Herman assured Sissy.

"You had better because I promise to chop off his lolly if I ever catch him by Mavis again. I know you help him fix her house."

"No, I am the one who give Mavis a help."

"You lie for him because you want him help you now. Man, you taking chances. You know Lorna don't play, eh?"

"Hurry, it's getting late," Herman urged Jacko.

Jacko removed a crank handle from under the driver's seat and mumbled something about his battery.

"Give it some gas," Jacko cranked vigorously and shouted to

Herman in the driver's seat. "Pull out the choke," he again shouted and continued cranking.

At last the truck sputtered and Jacko shouted to Herman in the cab of the truck, "Keep pumping! Give it gas!"

"It need two people to start this truck. How you does make out when you alone?" Herman teased.

"I thought all you wanted was for it to take you where you going," Jacko retorted.

Herman rushed upstairs and was dismayed to find nothing had been done in preparation for the journey.

"Where's your mammy?" he asked his eldest daughter Sophie.

"She went out," she replied.

"Where she said she was going?"

"I dunno. She didn't say. I see she leave in a truck."

Meanwhile Jacko had entered the room and appraised of the situation continued the inquiry. "She say how long she going for or when she coming back?"

Sophie shook her head. "You know if the same truck bringing her back?"

Twelve year-old Johnny joined the chatter showing off his knowledge of motor vehicles on the island.

"They have two new-kind Ford truck like it, but not the red one, the blue one. This one my mummy went in is T-156 and the other one is T-355."

"Un huh, saga boy Dennis," Jacko said dubiously for all to hear. Then he left the room.

Herman joined Jacko after a 30-minute interval. He was leaning on the iron railing of the second floor balcony viewing activity on the hostel grounds below.

"We leaving just now," Herman told Jacko.

"You mean you not waiting for your wife?"

"No!" Herman said sharply. "As a matter of fact, I am going with all the children and my belongings."

"Look, as a friend, I can wait or I will go and come back."

"You forget is my son in the police hands I am trying to get help for. If she don't give a damn because I told her to get ready while I am going to look for you to take us to see Miss Mable." I had a feeling she didn't want to go by Ma Baxter so she disappeared.

36

The Baxter sisters, Mable and Diana, had moved into the sprawling estate home of their brother, David, after the fire. Their sudden and widespread loss had thrown the sisters into sullen moods. They were left only with memories of the antique treasures and memorabilia that stood on the varnished pitch-pine floors and partitions on which hung past and present family pictures alongside each other in the heritage home of over sixty years.

The four Baxter siblings now spent lots of time together occupied in nostalgic recall, remembering teenage Baxter brothers forever in boisterous activity who were often extracting wood splinters from the soles of their feet and although fearing the burn of reddish-black liquid iodine applied to cuts and bruises by their parents, it did not lessen the many playtime scars on shins and chins. The many physical spats among playmates were of short duration and feelings of enmity soon dissolved. Weary parents often ordered boys out of the house on to safe streets and harmless sidewalks with orders to be home before sundown. Every year, they experienced upsetting moments of traditional de-worming during school holidays when they were made to ingest foul tasting purgative medicines.

Knowledge on the divine plan was imparted to upper-class daughters under an artifice of virginal goodness with its associated rewards. They were given dolls to groom and carry as sterile playmates and education was later channeled to home economics. The interaction with dolls was not a learning process related to later raising real babies. It was instead a matter of gender distinction through role-playing. In existing contrast elder daughters of lower class families took care of new additions to the family for a number of years.

The serious business of some domestic and conjugal decisions required permission of parents, and sanction by the parish priest. Awaiting a courtship was a melodramatic hit or miss affair and care had to be taken in acceptance of a suitor for acceptance of a partner in marriage, is indissoluble according to the laws of the Catholic Church.

37

The dissimilarity of lifestyles of the Baxter sisters was a redeeming feature. Diana was liberal and fond of children and often expressed empathy for the underprivileged. She rushed outside to attend to the group of children seated among the assorted packages on an open truck parked in front the iron gate of David Baxter's mansion home. Appearing soon after her was Lynette, always in a study of the everyday plight of lower-class citizens. She was shocked and agitated on hearing the stories from Herman of Victor's arrest and detention in police custody. She became agitated and was appalled on learning both aunts knew and kept the news of Victor's arrest away from her deliberately.

The normally sedate household of David Baxter was in turmoil with Lynette screaming at her aunts for withholding information on Victor, and David assailing Mable for inviting the Provident family to his home while Mable was managing the difficult task of wriggling out of David's accusation and at the same time scolding Lynette for her impolite manners with an unmistakably probing question.

"Why are you so upset when he is not even your type?"

Diana Baxter wrestled in a conscience appeaser asking everyone to be cognizant of a disaster that occurred in Tabor City. "It is circumstances surrounding this disaster that resulted in Mr. Provident son's arrest and this very unfortunate incident drew him this way to seek help for his son and not for any other reason," Diana argued.

There was partial success and before further argument reoccurred, Mrs. Judith Baxter, a noted socialite, claimed the floor. "Over the 25 years we have been married, David has been extremely generous in assisting groups involved in sports, culture and voluntary organizations. However, he despises those who try to abuse the goodness of others because they have been successful through sheer hard work."

38

Prior to the fire, Herman often sought advice from Miss Mable and would stop at the gate entrance to Baxter's Yard for this purpose. He was never shy or embarrassed to obtain her counsel. Miss Mable, likewise, was always disposed and willing, never too busy to offer gospel-based advice after hearing his confessions, especially those issues emanating out of relationships she was unlikely to encounter.

Herman needed Mable now more than ever. The distance and inconvenience of travel was no deterrent to the urge he felt to consult with Miss Mable on the most serious problem of his life, Victor's brush with the law. The dominant spirit of Miss Mable bonded respectfully with the manhood of a helpful and gentle acolyte.

They sat on the front porch in surroundings of botanical splendor. A late afternoon sun filtered through a solarium onto a newly enthused Herman Provident in private audience with Mable. Meanwhile, Diana was dutifully securing the rest of his family in an old trailer parked in the huge barn situated a hundred meters from the main residence. The social outlook at the mansion had cooled but tension was still above normal. Mable fired off two questions that did not help lower the temperature.

"Where's Lorna? Why is she not with you?"

Herman bowed his head and appeared to be making an effort to reply but she continued before he could get a word out. "I never told you, Herman, but Lorna speaks to me in an offhand way and I find acts in an unfriendly manner towards me." She paused, though not long enough for Herman to reply.

"Not that I care one way or the other," Mable added nonchalantly. She looked relieved not to have to interact with Lorna in Baxter's Yard anymore.

A reply from Herman seemed of no importance, as well as her next statement was a lecture on decorum. "Your son should know you do not abuse the police. If only he had politely explained the coincidence of having a suitcase of new clothes. Why did he think he would get away with an act like that?"

"Maybe he was angry at the time with me because I said he should have been on the boat to England." Herman looked and sounded remorseful.

"But you are perfectly correct." Mable paused and leaned back in her chair. "He does not have your temperament," she said comfortingly. She paused again before leaning forward. "He is everything like his mother, discourteous and pigheaded."

Herman's eyes looked around for an appealing flower to mollify the jabbing pain of this assessment. She was noting his unease after pointing out displeasing aspects in a family he had done his best to foster as a model of stability. She looked at him and anticipated his main purpose for the visit; a wry smile wrinkled her cheeks.

"Yes, yes, yes I had a chat with the Attorney General when I heard what occurred with Victor. Mrs. Baxter contacted him for me and he said he will attend to it first thing in the morning."

Herman clasped his hands and bowed three times, "Thank you, thank you, and thank you!"

39

Everyone reasoned Lynette had removed herself from present company and was still fretting over being left in the dark about the events surrounding Victor. She now reappeared assisting Diana in preparing some meals for the Provident family. A student of psychology observing the change from near hysteria to a self assured and animated posture would know something had occurred during the interval. However, it was seldom a concern when change was supportive and was lending a helping hand. Lynette was doing everything to maintain a modest composure even as she considered her plan in motion to free Victor while others in the household were still diffident.

During their return after serving meals to the Provident clan, Lynette stepped in front of Diana preventing her further movement.

"I have something to tell you Aunty D.," Lynette began. "I think I managed to get Victor out of prison."

Diana mildly raised her eyebrows and tilted her head.

Lynette went on. "I think by tonight Victor will no longer be a prisoner."

"But he is not a prisoner. He is not sentenced by a court of law. Right now he is a suspect being held in police custody pending further investigation, then perhaps prosecution if the Attorney General finds there is sufficient evidence to proceed." Diana resumed walking. She was trying to spare Lynette's feeling and dispel ludicrous fantasies of being able to get Victor released.

"Okay, okay, Aunty D., I agree, what I really want to tell you is that I phoned my friend's father who knows me because of his son Tom and guess who he is, the Commissioner of Police William Blyth. Can you imagine, me telling the Chief of Police his men were wrong to arrest Victor?"

"But he was on the wharf and, and, you mean up to now he does not know Victor was arrested? I find that hard to believe."

"Well, he did promise to go down to the station and sort the matter out right away."

"Did he?"

"He sounded genuine and as you pointed out he was on the wharf among those saying goodbye and knows Victor through his son Tom."

"Let's hope you are right and not engaging in wishful thinking," remarked a skeptical Diana.

Lynette blocked Diana's path again in peaceful confrontation.

"But I am not finished giving you the full story. Of course you know the hospital surgeon, Dr. Keswick. Do you know his son's best friend is Victor?"

"School friends do not necessarily mean social companionship outside school hours," Diana said.

"On the contrary, it went further than that. He's lived at Vivian Keswick's home for the last six months," informed Lynette.

"Isn't Vivian the one people say is a classical scholar and whiz kid at math?" Diana asked.

"That is why you should ask why Victor is his close friend. So you see, people don't know how bright Victor is because of who he is."

"Don't tell me you want to involve Dr. Keswick in this fiasco?"

"Aunty D., he was more than happy to help, his wife is the one who got the clothes for Victor, which is why it was so expensive looking. Do you know the wife is an heiress?"

"Do you know a young girl like you should not be getting involved in too many things that don't concern you and are over your head?" Diana's voice was stern as she stepped briskly, unlikely to be stopped in her tracks before reaching the house.

40

Lorna was engrossed in deciding how within the allotted time she would complete both missions. This ongoing dilemma had forced a choice on Lorna to either rush back to the hostel to join Herman for the journey to the Baxter estate or continue to the police station hoping to see Victor. The latter held more immediate prospects and emotional satisfaction.

"I come to look for my son. Where you holding my son, my first child?"

The strident voice turned every head, its tone was imperious and impertinent, and everyone sat up because it came over as menacing and fearless.

"He not a criminal. He went to college, he graduate with more brains than all of you!"

All counter and desk police of all ranks remained glued to their seats. Very rarely were women arrested and the policemen on duty had never taken a female into custody and hoped such action could be avoided. Presently there were no women prisoners on the island of Au Tabor and there were no female members of the local police force.

The maleness of the office was evident in a noticeably untidy dust laden environment and a stale unhygienic smell wafting across the room towards the entrance doorway presumably from out of sight toilets and prison cells.

In a nearby holding cell, Victor could hear his mother's voice and he fixed his lips to call out to her but suddenly felt apprehensive. He didn't want to add to her distress.

"Look, I bring food for my child because I sure you all starving him," Lorna said urgently.

Hearing this, Victor relented. In a plaintive voice, he said loud enough for her to hear, "Mama just give it to them and tell them bring it for me."

"Victor my child, that's you? Victor, Victor, why they doing that to you?"

Heartfelt emotion intensified to hysterical behavior and was proving difficult to control. The policemen stood around hoping the weeping and bawling would soon lessen as it was attracting a crowd of passersby. Out of this gathering crowd were a welcome couple of womenfolk who immediately wrapped consoling arms around her collapsing body.

"Please, please, my son, don't do nobody nothing," she cried gasping between loud sobs."

"What's going on here?" a voice of authority rang out above the commotion. Chief of Police William Blyth had just arrived, and his presence made the on-duty police staff spring into action to clear the crowd. To restore order and calm, one officer took the meal into Victor and another one promised Lorna to permit a meeting with her son as soon as he was through eating.

There was relative calm following those promises and the chief moved urgently to an inner section of the office and engaged two senior officers in conversation.

"I have been receiving many calls suggesting the young man has been wrongly apprehended and we're in support of releasing him." Police Chief Blyth informed the officers.

"We too have had many people come in here claiming to know him and his family and that we got the wrong person," added the sergeant.

"What have you all charged him with?" Chief Blyth asked the sergeant.

"Disorderly behavior and resisting arrest," was the reply.

"By the way, was he among those thugs who wanted to beat up my son during carnival?"

"No, sir."

"But most of them were his hooligan friends."

"I would attest to that, sir."

A front desk staff interrupted and excitedly announced that Dr. Richard Keswick was at the counter with a lawyer.

"What does he want?" a surprised chief Blyth turned and looked toward the counter.

"Hi Bill, I'm glad you're here. Just the man I want to see," the naming was loud and salient.

Chief William Blyth moved promptly to the counter and invited Dr. Keswick to a private corner of the office.

"Tell me, Doc. How can I help? I hope it's nothing too serious."

"Serious enough. I refer to the matter of Victor Provident wrongly accused of stealing. Such arbitrary and wrongful arrest could cause long-term psychological injury. Normally, I thought you would have reacted sooner with your knowledge of the young man's circumstances and the causes for his distress. I really should not have had to bring my lawyer. He is here as a precautionary measure. If a negotiated release fails, we can offer bail as an alternative."

Chief Blyth had stopped listening before the monologue ended.

His eyes shifted rapidly in an evasive side-to-side movement.

"How could you have known the process for his release was being discussed when you walked in? His mother's behavior caused some minor disruption and attracted a crowd but as you quite rightly observed it was necessary for me to provide to my men the information why an unconditional release would serve as vindication for this misunderstanding." Chief Blyth explained in unnecessary detail.

"Am I to assume the process is complete and the wrongly accused is free to accompany me out of this Police Station?" Dr. Keswick sought confirmation.

Chief Blyth did not reply directly, but turned to face the general office and in his powerful voice shouted, "Corporal Jones, release the prisoner! Do you have the keys? The prisoner is to be released forthwith."

It was obvious that the supportive crowd just outside the building heard the welcome order when they surged into the station behind Lorna. Emotional scenes played outside the station for almost half an hour during which Victor related experiences of his arrest that began to stir indignation among the crowd. Lorna's faith in the Almighty was considerably strengthened and she challenged the crowd. "Now tell me if is not the hand of God that send the doctor here to free my son."

Dr. Keswick then declared it time to depart and surprised the crowd with the news that he would be arranging for Victor to rejoin his colleagues in England. Lorna was overjoyed.

"Doctor, you are a good man and God will bless you for what you are doing," she began in an impromptu speech of thanks. "You are not like the hypocrites that always playing they want to help my husband and family."

Victor stepped up and put an arm around his mother in a gentle effort to end further recrimination. She relented partly but cautioned, "Boy don't be like your father and be soft for them to take advantage. I runnin now to tell him the news."

Lorna headed to the barrack residence confident she had resolved an issue that was the work of someone who conspired with the devil to have Victor arrested. She expected her husband to be in a bad mood awaiting her for an undertaking no longer necessary. In its place she rehearsed how she would announce to her family the exciting news before anyone of them uttered a word, "Victor is free, he is out, he is with Dr. Keswick back in his old home."

Lorna pictured the family jumping around happily elated by the news. Right at that moment, her back ached and she wanted to sprawl out on a mattress on the floor before they asked for the details, although she believed Herman would be anxious to get the details and would be leading the inquiry after his initial anger.

Lorna did not see a problem in showing how divine intervention defeated the evil forces. A prime example seemed to her, the chance she took riding in a truck with a stranger. She would point out how this caused her unexpectedly to enter church, to pray and bump into Father Limos. The prayer he gave her with his words, "the strength and courage to overcome all evil" was an awareness by Father Limos some evil was at work.

Further two important people, Police Chief Blyth and Dr. Keswick became involved in Victor's release. Lorna believed this fact would make her husband glow with satisfaction.

Lorna had never walked so far so fast in unfamiliar surroundings. She felt very tired and about to collapse but was able to muster reserve energy with present thoughts of rejoining her family with the welcome news.

A next-door resident in the common balcony, which spanned the full length of the building, was the first person with whom Lorna came into contact.

"Well, well you all back, I thought you all would be gone for a long time seeing how you left the place empty."

Lorna stood and looked at their empty room, turned and without a word gave her neighbor a blank stare and then crumpled into a heap on the concrete floor.

41

Miss Mable said the prayer of "Grace before meals" ahead of a sumptuous dinner spread the five Baxter family members were about to partake. The elegant setting of cutlery and crystal dinnerware glittered and sparkled beneath a twenty light candelabra chandelier.

Judith Baxter was endeavoring to turn away the memory of losses suffered in the fire by her sisters in law Mable and Diana Baxter. To cheer them up she tried entertaining with lavish and sophisticated social activity such as impromptu tea parties and bridge sessions with invited influential friends. However an unimpressed Miss Mable was adamant the inferno was a warning sign and suggested instead the gathering meet in prayer.

Everybody was seated and served by maids in starched apron uniforms. The telephone was ringing and Mrs. Baxter directed the closest maid to take the call. The maid put down the receiver and walked to Lynette's side and spoke in a barely audible voice.

"It's for you, Miss Lynette," the maid said. "Must I tell the gentleman you will call back after supper?" The maid felt this would impress others at the table.

"No, no I will take it," Lynette said, reaching for the phone and immediately gave out a loud squeal that momentarily got everyone's attention. "It's Victor! They released him and he's free!"

On the phone, Victor was effusive in thanking her for the part she played as relayed to him by Dr. Keswick. Lynette returned to the table clapping her hands applauding the occasion of Victor's release.

"Aunty D., you see it worked," she said to the room.

The reaction around the table could only be interpreted as indifferent. No one looked up or gave the faintest sign of acknowledgement. Lynette stood silently for a moment, alertly snapped her fingers, then she turned and ran out the house to meet with the Provident family in the garage.

"Hello, hello, hello, good news, good news. Victor is free!"

No one in the family appeared excited by Lynette's clarion call. The intended high point of the news was received with an unresponsive gloom around the family.

"Victor is free," Lynette said again. "He was released this evening." This was not the effect she expected the news to have.

"You must be very happy to know that your brother is now free." The faces gathered at the entrance displayed expressions of distrust although an effort was made to share in the excitement Lynette exuded and some smiles appeared all around.

"Where's Victor? Why didn't you bring him?" eleven year-old Agatha asked.

"She knows him well," claimed twelve year-old Johnny. "You used to talk to him from upstairs Miss Mable house."

Herman looked on pensively. He displayed the emotions of someone unsure of the message and the messenger.

"Have you told your aunty because she was making arrangements with your uncle to go to the police station tomorrow?" Herman asked.

"Yes, I just told her he has been released."

This news pre-empted Herman's plan to demonstrate his influence with higher-ups in Tabor City.

"Do you know if they let him go for good?" Herman asked, still not convinced of the handling at the level explained by Lynette.

"Dr. Keswick signed for his release, so I suppose he will be responsible for him."

"So Dr. Keswick have him as his houseboy?"

Lynette was upset and disappointed by the reception and comment. "Why are you saying things like that when you know better? He will have a comfortable place to stay."

Lynette showed disgust and turned to go back to the house but Herman stopped her. "Lynette, I didn't mean it in a bad way if he is houseboy. They sometimes used to call me your aunty houseboy. Do you know if his mother was with him?"

"He told me his mother was hurrying home to give you all a full account of what happened. Wait, but how is she planning to get here? Anyway I have to hurry back, I was just having my supper." And with that, Lynette ran off without an answer to her question.

42

Lorna's neighbors at the hostel were unsure of what caused her to collapse and decided to send her to the hospital when they were unable to contact family members. Doctors examined her and found no symptoms of illness. So they sedated her and scheduled additional tests for the next morning.

The doctors next morning concluded Lorna had suffered extreme mental and physical exhaustion and she was discharged and advised to get some rest. But Lorna needed a starting point, a reference to get herself back on track – a beginning to help her plan the next step. Her mind was adrift in a land vacant of home and family. She got some reprieve from her pleasant memories as a resident of the former sanctuary of Baxter's Yard and the support and goodwill of neighbors.

However a dark cloud of evil floated lurid images of Iris into the forefront of her mind. She spent the day alone in the hostel room planning her next move and gathering overwhelming facts in support of vengeance for the numerous hardships she suffered recently. She counted them in her mind, starting with the fire that burned down her home, Victor not leaving for school and his ensuing arrest, and then the separation from her family and her recent hospital stay.

Lorna was adamant about the question she would ask every former Baxter's Yard resident she meet, "Has anyone seen Iris since the fire?"

Although Iris was never a favorite of the residents of Baxter's Yard, as a longstanding resident, her oddity was etched on the memory of every former resident. Her only 'sins' were to stoutly refuse to be socially accessible and show disdain for the conduct of some neighbors. Remarkably, no one could remember seeing her just before, during or after the fire but there was a desire to know her fate. There were expressions of melodrama in recall when former residents met with Lorna.

"I believe her disappearing have a lot to do with how the fire start," a former resident offered.

"Why is it is de same night when Victor had to leave, de place catch fire to stop him leaving," Ma Reggie tried to interpret for Lorna what she meant with a mystified look on her face.

"My dear if you looking for enemies you don't have to look far. If you remember from the start I did warn you." Bajan Tilley dolefully gave her opinion.

The reckoning of former residents typified the real story of Baxter's Yard as an arena of communal incitement and excitement with its vituperative exchanges rising to the brink of physical conflict.

Lorna was determined to remain on the prowl for both Iris and her attendant spirit thing. After collecting her personal belongings from the hostel, Lorna lacked the means of contacting her husband and children in the secluded and exclusive estate of the Baxters. She decided the following morning to head to the hills to be with her family of mother, sisters and brothers. There was a brother in particular whom she believed could unravel and repel the attacks on herself and family.

"Woh Miss Lorna, is so long I ain't see you, you coming back to live here?" greeted a long-time resident.

Lorna was walking up a steep road next to a large retaining wall supporting land on which stood two newly built houses near the edge. She looked up at the houses and offered an uncertain reply,

"Maybe, I might, I dunno."

"Ay, ay, look sister Lorna coming up the hill," shouted her Sister Karen.

"The children with her?" a voice from inside the house inquired, "No, Mama she is alone."

"Dat's a bad sign."

"Mama Nita you and your signs," Karen said scornfully rising from a basin of soaking clothes and methodically swiping soap suds off her arms and wraps them around Lorna.

"What happen, sis? You not looking happy?"

"Too many things happening."

"Like what?"

Lorna ignored the question and moved with purpose to the door where six nephews and nieces, ages four to eleven years, children of two sisters and a brother, were dancing and shouting,

"Aunty Lorna, Aunty Lorna, Aunty what you bring for me? Where the sweeties?"

"The big fire burn all the sweeties."

"Why you didn't bring the children with you?" asked the eleven year-old.

Lorna took a deep breath, hugged each one and softly exhaled, "Next time I will bring them."

The children were shooed away by Karen and Mamma Nita to give Lorna a chance to settle down and relax.

"Do you want juice or some tea, lime squash or lemon tea?"

"Juice, but I want hot cocoa tea for later."

Among trusted family on the hill and though her legs ached, Lorna felt she had physically and mentally climbed the hill and reached a safe haven that sheltered her from childhood.

"Send and call the boys," Mama Nita ordered. She usually was apprehensive that a tragic situation was imminent and was early with the panic button.

"Mama, today is Friday and the afternoon nearly over." Karen calmed Mama Nita with the expectation that everybody usually made their way home on Fridays.

Jonas was the eldest in his late forties and was on his way home from the forest. He holstered his cutlass upside down with the blade resting along his forearm; a bulky canvas haversack slung across his chest and his face was passive beneath the frizzled brim of a large straw hat. He was in step with his donkey as it led him up a narrow track. Without a given command the donkey halted when it got to an open space in front a thatched roof shed next to the family home. Four bags of charcoal were being offloaded from the donkey when Lorna came around to greet Jonas. She stood silently a few yards away and when Jonas turned and saw her, an inquiring frown quickly changed into a wide-mouthed grin.

"Lorna, dat is you?" he shouted.

Lorna smiled and laughed delightfully. "How are you Jonas?"

"What you doing up here," he asked in a welcoming voice.

Lorna hugged Jonas, ignoring that question for a second time.

"I dirty, I dirty," warned Jonas, but Lorna did not let go right away.

"You alone here? No one else come with you?"

Lorna shook her head and choked on this question for a third time. Jonas noticed the gloom as it rolled over her face and proposed, "Well, we going to prepare big fete to welcome you."

43

Lorna was hurting given her semblance of a prodigal daughter returning alone to relations on the hill after many years. The family members lived within a ten-minute walk from each other except for Lorna, the only one legitimately married, and so having arrived without her husband and children was disconcerting.

Jonas had three children with a woman he visited occasionally but resided in the family home along with his mother and sister Karen.

Sonia, an attractive lady of East Indian heritage, was introduced to Lorna as Donald's latest live-in girlfriend. Sonia made a good first impression on Lorna when she expressed an all-embracing welcome.

"I have heard so much about you and your lovely family, Donald talks about you all the time and he always promising to take me to see you. I believe you must be his favorite?"

"You think so," Lorna could hardly contain her delight. "He just says so because I am the only one not around all the time. Where is he?" demanded Lorna.

"He has somebody with him and he says he will come as soon as he is finished."

Donald, the youngest son, operated a nameless business organization. He had an office catering to clients wishing to discuss or request advice for any imaginable problem. No one had been able to convincingly explain how he was able to acquire such a large building formerly owned by a deceased prominent but eccentric lawyer whom he worked for as a messenger. Through his work, he was also able to gain limited knowledge of legal niceties however incomplete.

And so it was a hug and reenactment of ring-a-ring-a-roses and the cheerfulness drew all the family and children outside to witness the joyous expressions of a reunion between brother Donald and sister Lorna.

Hilton a shopkeeper, Mike a barber and Jane a maid arrived together and Donald immediately appraises the gathering with a favorable welcome.

"Welcome to the Alcides and Pascals, the happiest, most prosperous family in the world," Donald said, inflating the family's fortunes. The boys all signed as Alcides, the father's surname, but the girls opted for Pascal, the surname of their unmarried mother after the father left the household and moved to another part of Au Tabor in a relationship with another woman.

The Friday evening family gathering learnt surprisingly of a gilded reason to justify a celebration. In addition to Lorna's surprise visit, Mama Nita would be celebrating her golden jubilee that coming Sunday marking fifty years since she made her first communion. There were make-believe noises by the family for equal treatment of the celebrants and Mama Nita was cautioned to not delay future notifying of events.

Preparation for the fete began with excited bustle throughout Saturday. Various roles had been assigned for food preparation, drinks and music. Some friends and relatives were notified but the rest of hillside community would decide whether they might and wished to invite themselves. A number of factors could disqualify attendance, such as a recent dispute with a family member, unacceptable standard of hygiene and dress, and disorderly behavior. There are four robust brothers ready to ensure the self-invitees followed the norms of the hillside community.

44

The six Provident children camping with their father were in no mood to cooperate in any housekeeping chores in this makeshift accommodation of farm workers quarters. The hosts, represented by Diana Baxter, were very gracious; however, the attention raised suspicion among the children. The motherly attention made the children feel an attempt was being made to replace their real mother. As a result, their questions were straightforward and concise and rephrased down the ages.

"Have you seen my mother?"

"Where's my mammy?"

"I want my mammy."

Diana Baxter was defensive with her responses. "Have you asked your daddy? He's your mother's best friend and they know each other very well."

"But why she is not here with us?" asked Sophie, the eldest.

"Your daddy is the best person to ask that. I can't tell you why."

Sophie rejected Diana's defense and rattled her with an accusation. "You can't tell me why because you do not want to help my daddy to find my mommy."

Infuriated, Diana walked away and said nothing more. Diana had championed the family cause but with the latest clash support for the predicament of the Provident family dissipated and a meeting of the Baxter family was convened. An edict was issued by the family requiring the Provident clan to return to the hostel forthwith keeping the objective of a reunion with Lorna in the forefront. The Baxter family would provide all the support resources and services including transportation to ensure fulfillment of efforts to locate Lorna.

Herman accepted politely the decision as his best opportunity in the circumstances albeit the only one before him.

45

Even though living in the comparative luxury of Dr. Keswick's Pine Grove residence, Victor was unwilling to regard Baxter's Yard as less habitable. He reflected on Pine Grove as comparatively lifeless, humorless, without soul and human warmth. He recalled especially, being arrested in a similar type neighborhood and still had qualms when stepping outside. Irrespective of such sentiment, his insight elucidated and judgment was uplifted in the serenity and idyllic scene of cheery gardens with colorful blossoms lining neat and orderly walkways.

That Saturday morning, Victor planned to visit with his family and Dr. Keswick showed approval by going off his route to drop Victor at the hostel where his family had temporarily settled.

Victor was directed to the second floor and bounded up the steps in rising anticipation. There was no answer when he knocked on the door and peering through the glass window saw the room was empty. Only children were seen playing on the balcony. "The mister they have nobody living there," one confirmed.

"Where's your mother and father," Victor addressed the children with authority, "call one of them for me," he added before any could respond.

"I going and call my mother for you," a boy who appeared to be the eldest went in search.

"Hello, yes, can I help you?"

"My name is Victor Provident and I —"

"Oh yes, your mummy spoke so much about you," the woman said, interrupting Victor in a high voice. "I can see the resemblance."

"I thought she would be here with the rest of my family, do you know where they went to?"

The woman seemed quite capable of handling delicate situations. She had a strong physical presence, tall and buxom and of a mixed racial quality making it possible to identify or crossover into numerous ethnic groups. She was silent for an unusually long time, not knowing the answer or where the story began. "That fire had separated so many families and caused so much hardship," she began after a pause. "Your mother was so exhausted when she reached here on Thursday evening from God knows where, we had to take her to hospital."

"Hospital, you said?" Victor asked, trying to stay calm.

He watched as she nodded her head without a word.

"And did my father and the children," Victor continued. "Did they accompany her to the hospital?"

The woman realized she needed a way out of the conversation.

"You know I wish I could help, but I know neither your father nor the children were in the building when she arrived and this may have contributed to her fainting."

"She fainted?" Victor asked, now completely alarmed.

"She collapsed right before us and we then helped her. But don't worry she said she was feeling much better when she came back after being discharged yesterday morning."

"So where is she or where did she go to?" Victor paused longer after each word and lifted his voice a decibel in frustration.

The woman began in a sharper tone of voice. "All I know is when your mother returned from hospital, she picked up her things and said she was going to meet her brothers and sisters and we said goodbye. And, goodbye to you, Sir."

"Could you please tell me your name so I can mention it to my mother?" he hastily requested as the lady walked away.

She stopped, turned and said vaguely, "Tell her it's the lady in the room next door who took her to hospital after she collapsed."

46

A strategic meeting was in progress at Donald Alcide's office. Donald reclined pompously onto a flowered cloth cushion hitched to the high backrest of a wicker rocking chair. A bookshelf, overflowing with paperbacks and third-hand tattered volumes, spanned the full width of the partition behind him in a simulation of his former employer's office as a learned jurist. A room to the side with a half-drawn curtain allows a glimpse of the strange implements and skeletal bone sections used in his professed capability to discern and unravel any problem.

Also in attendance were the three other Alcide brothers listening to Lorna unload the woeful tale of suffering she had endured over the previous few days. Lorna enumerated those incidents she earlier recalled in the room following her return from hospital. She connected events to the peculiar ways of "one Miss Iris who used to live in Baxter's Yard and nobody knew where she livin now." She gave hearsay examples of Iris delving in works of evil using her powers to do harm to others. Lorna then handed over to Donald who with the skill of an impresario and chilling voice intonations he wrapped many yarns around his attentive audience.

"Au Tabor has at least seven kind of spirits, some are like jumbies. Others are ordinary persons with power like some priests, and some obeah persons but not all do good work and remove evil spirits. Others are Gens-Caches like the wicked 'Gardeurs,' and evil 'Diablesse,' 'Soucouyant,' 'Papa-Bois,' 'Magi-Noirs.' I can tell you story after story about those devil spirits l have had to face."

Donald paused, took a deep breath and then continued. "From what you tell me sister, is a Soucouyant you facing and is the hardest one to destroy because it can fly after the lady shed her skin. If you can put some hot spice like pepper and garlic and things like that in the empty skin it will not be able to put it back on because it will burn it; that is one way to catch it. If at night you see something like a bat flying; that could be it. Or if you see a ball of flame moving across the sky; that could be it too. You say nobody have seen her since the fire," Donald did not await confirmation, "that strange nobody know where she move to after the fire. Well first we have to find out where she hiding." Donald glanced individually at his three brothers as he spoke.

"Could a Soucouyant when it's a ball of flame start a fire like the other night?" Lorna asked.

"That is very easy for it to do," Donald verified straight away.

"I remember Mr. Baxter who the sugar estate belong to saying during the fire it was like a force from away and no one could see it to fight it."

"That is Soucouyant for you," said Donald approvingly.

"Oh maybe the fire burnt her empty shell before the soucouyant had time to get back inside it that's why nobody have seen her."

"I was thinking about that already," Donald disingenuously said. "But let us give attention to the fete for tomorrow and don't worry after that I will fix everything."

47

Herman and the six children met with a Baxter family adviser around midday at the hostel and were updated on Lorna's whereabouts. Neighbors, now curious, were up-to-date on all the Provident family's business.

Herman, still protective of his image, greeted his next-door neighbors at the hostel with the impression he was away on overnight business. "I am sorry to have given you all this trouble. I had planned to be back sooner after attending to some business, but thanks anyway for taking care of Lorna." His tone of regret indicated all was well and nothing untoward had occurred. He made no secret of his plans to join his wife at her family home on Hillside and accepted greetings on her behalf. Hostel residents were happy to learn of the planned reunion.

New arrangements were being made for the unexpected trip to the Hillside district with support promised by the Baxter family. Unfortunately, last minute cancellation of assistance was ordered by the Baxter family when they learned their vehicle and employees would be entering the Hilltop neighborhood. The mission was considered a risk of exposure with long-range security threat. It was feared the amorphous character of this uncivil community only needed the opportunity of a toehold to spread out to the region of the Baxter plantation.

It would now require Herman to arrange transportation and to go forward with the trip to join his wife. He was surprisingly comforted by a sense of his newfound autonomy. He knew he could rely on his friend Jacko who incidentally lived in the area of Hillside.

Herman learned of distress on arriving at the hostel and finding no one there. He lowered his head and drew down his shoulders with hands clasped behind his back. The Baxter's Yard syndrome of involvement with police and prison had stained his family from two separate locations, though he had worked diligently to prevent this from ever happening. He wanted to protect his family from this infection that had afflicted many within the Yard and was convinced it was a contagion native to the Baxter Yard district that stuck to those afflicted and nothing he believed could have prepared Victor for his predicament with the police.

48

Victor was rushing back to the hospital intent on finding out more about his mother's location and condition. He was prepared to use his privileged position with Dr. Keswick if necessary. Victor felt assured it was just exhaustion combined with severe stress and a period of rest was recommended. But his anxiety about his mother's state was not lessened. He was determined to travel to Hillside to see her, convinced he had contributed to her stress and was now in a position to bring about relief through his visit.

It was close to the midday hour and Victor, hoping Dr. Keswick would be going home for lunch, decided to wait around the hospital. While standing by the car, he saw a group of former Baxter Yard friends, Blackie, Planche and Colom approaching the hospital compound. The sight of the three old pals made him feel hesitant although happy to see them after some time. His present social life had affected relationships with them, but Victor was concerned foremost with the reason they were together entering the hospital compound. Victor nevertheless ran out excitedly to greet them and any apprehension was put aside by Colom, "Man you are just the one we looking for."

Victor looked around at the faces of the other two friends for a hint in any form of what Colom meant.

"Boy, you don't know who very sick in there we going to see," Colom continued.

Planche had no time for dramatic effect and piped in, "Miss Iris."

"Yes man," Colom added incredulously. Noticing the surprised look on Victor's face, Colom went on. "Maybe you can ask your doc to take a look and see if he can help."

The request made Victor uneasy and protective of his relationship with Dr. Keswick. He figured his best argument would be an ethical one. "I do not think it is right for me to make that request of a doctor at a hospital where he is expected to do all he can to help."

Blackie, always the instigator pounced. "But it was right for the doc to ask for bail for you when they had lock up your backside, eh?"

Colom, the fact-finder, chastised Blackie. "Easy, Blackie. The man not guilty so they were bound to free him up even without bail."

"But Colom, the man forever backing off and playing goodie, goodie, so much so they arrest him and that never happen to any if us."

"Because you always stay where you belong, Blackie," Colom replied sarcastically.

"Maybe he can just mention to the doc he know Miss Iris and help will come," Planche tried again.

"Man, Planche is not magic doin in there. Tings don't happen just so. Either Victor goin help or he not goin help." Colom put it as a matter of conscience for Victor.

"When fellas reach a certain place they does forget where they came from," Blackie maintained.

"Fellas, let us go see Miss Iris before she make it to the next side," urged Planche.

Meanwhile, Victor left to obtain the wardroom where Miss Iris was located and they soon followed him. The three faces of concern for the welfare of Miss Iris were not unlike the faces of the jeering teenagers who had engaged in mischief and ran away after throwing stones on the roof of Miss Iris's house. They made their claim for assistance an undisputed right, aiming to be declared heroes in the care and recovery of Miss Iris's health.

At Iris's bedside were two nuns standing behind best friend Miss Winifred who was seated and leaning forward peering into the patient's face. On the opposite side of the bed, a nurse stood with both hands holding a raised bed sheet waiting for Miss Winifred to move her head out of the way before covering Miss Iris's entire body.

"I wanted to be sure she had nothing more to say," Miss Winifred explained as the body was being wheeled away.

The moment of silence surrounding the group ended with a snivel by Miss Winifred who then intoned three times words she claimed were the last uttered by Miss Iris. "There is a space, there is space, and yes there is space."

The nuns stood in silence until one intoned, "Let us pray for the soul of Iris and of the faithful departed."

She then addressed the four young men. "The response is 'Lord have mercy on us."

A startled look on the four faces seemed an admission of their unsuitability for this role. It was the first time the four young men witnessed a final hour and were apparently humbled by the experience. The usual toughness changed to a demeanor of penitents who had come to pay homage and seek a reprieve. They sneaked glances at the beds with patients lining the room but quickly looked away when the faces afflicted with pain and frailty stared back. Feelings of guilt evident in their reaction crept over them, mindful of the envious effect their healthy youthful presence could have on the bedridden.

As the nuns were leaving, Miss Winifred thanked them profusely for the assurance that burial arrangements would be taken care of by the nuns.

"Iris's vagabonds appear terrified and don't fit the picture I had from what Iris used to tell me." Miss Winifred introduced herself with an exposé of the four teenagers.

"Why were you all making her life miserable?"

"It was not only us but even the big people used to quarrel with her all the time." Planche wanted to share any faultfinding.

"I dunno nothing about that, eh," dissented Blackie annoyingly.

"She was different and she never mixed with the rest of the people and I suppose they did not like that," offered Victor.

"Oh is that why you wanted to see her on her dying bed so you can report what you saw to them," Miss Winifred challenged.

"Dying Miss!" exclaimed Colom, we never thought of her as dying, we had not seen her since after the fire."

"Tell them all she wanted was her own space to live her life and tell them don't use you all but come themselves if they want to find out something."

"No Miss nobody sent us, we came on our own." Blackie tried to convince her.

"Tell them she died peacefully and you all can bear witness there was nothing strange happening."

"Yes Miss we will tell them but believe no one sent us and so who must we say spoke to us," Planche felt he was more credible.

"I am an ex-teacher, maybe you don't know me and never heard of me, but I taught all of them, your mothers, fathers, aunties, so I know all of them, just tell them Teacher Winnie is the one who spoke to you."

49

Day four at sea, the monotony of bedtime and mealtime clocks watching an endless ocean of water curling and frothing past the hull of the steamer, and the anxiety of an unknown and uncertain future, caused hearts and minds to replay chapters of a past life on Au Tabor.

Zane at breakfast that Sunday morning and made a surprise request that had been a module of past daily life at school and formal assemblies in Au Tabor.

"Please stand for prayers," Zane requested with a cleric's authority. On impulse the other three friends stood up without hesitation maybe in part because elderly couples at adjacent tables heard.

"Lord God who created the heavens and the earth. Fill our hearts and minds with kindness and fairness. Help us love our neighbor as we love ourselves. Give us strength to gather our daily bread in your name so we may forever spread your gospel across the land. Forever and ever, Amen. Oh Lord don't forget to help Tom get over his seasickness."

They all laughed in relief and delayed comment on Zane's newly acquired authority. However after breakfast and a decent pause, no one was surprised when the challenge for divinity student Zane was submitted by Tom who has never ceased in an attempt to get even.

"As a young Catholic, I was taught there is no way one could go directly to Heaven without spending some time in purgatory. We had to atone for venial sin, a result of a disobedient act of Adam and Eve, the parents of all mankind. I am given to understand the punishment calls for the compulsory wearing of clothes or more specifically the covering of our genitals." Tom held his gaze on Zane as he continued; "It is supposedly the reason we do not possess the natural instinct to go naked as is the choice of other primates. Many attribute the decision to wear clothes as a sign of intelligence, hence you will find nudity most prevalent among tribes in the jungle."

Tom paused but no one felt inclined to fill in on godly matters so he continued. "My question is, are we getting closer to completing the term of our sentence and will we achieve full atonement on completion of our term."

"Perhaps we should be granted an indicator of which future generation will walk the earth naked." Tom made this assessment as a strikingly attractive lady passenger sauntered nearby. The distraction caused a short pause of the review but he recovered in style.

"Here is a possible case to dispute; hemlines are rising, inching up every decade and after uncovering the ankle bone, they have climbed and barely cover the kneecap."

An indifferent chuckle came from among the other students.

"I am prepared to wager that within six decades dress hems will have reached above the thighs. Any bets?" Tom tried to stir controversy out of lackluster company.

"Yes, if you mean now. I am not going to wait sixty years for my winnings."

There was convivial laughter. It was assumed that Vivian, the son of English born parents, would use his kinship to make the initial contact with the captain and some officers. The rapport was enhanced by the second cricket test in progress between England and the West Indies at Lords. The students were granted the facility of a special room with speakers relaying ball-by-ball commentary on the match. This was a welcome treat for an activity-starved group. We were joined by some English passengers and a partisan atmosphere soon developed into a cordial debate on whether the game was best approached in a calypso or urbane style. Then the commentator said he had an important announcement to make, "A special collection is being made for the victims of a devastating fire that razed the capital city on the West Indian island of Au Tabor. Please give generously. Many of you are unaware that the armband worn by the West Indian players is an emblem of condolence."

After the announcement the four students felt constricted without a casualty and damage update and suddenly developed guilt feelings as they had been without anxiety until then. Tom immediately retired to his room with a severe attack of seasickness, and the others sprang into action.

Vivian managed to salvage some used cans and turned them into coin boxes to collect donations from crew and passengers. Martin collected used clothing from passengers and crew and had asked the captain to transport it to Au Tabor on his return trip. Zane insisted everyone should attend a session to offer prayers for the welfare of the victims.

The cooperation received on day five from captain and crew was a clear indication that they had anticipated earlier signs of distressed behavior from the students having sailed while the fire was raging.

50

After holy mass that Sunday in the Hillside community church situated on the highest elevation, the men lingered nearby and showed no signs of discomfort by remaining in funeral-black suits under a mid-morning sun. Male heads uncovered inside the church promptly donned felt hats as they came out the church doors. The women in calf-length dresses and stylish hats were still mopping their brows with tiny embroidered handkerchiefs and twirled accordion fans close to their faces. Some expertly opened umbrellas to shield the sun's rays while hurrying home to escape the heat.

The men stood their ground and then shuffled noticeably in the direction of the rum shops where banter soon recorded higher animated noise levels. After leaving the imposing church structure the men spent considerably more time in the ramshackle hut across the road where the server in a vest and shorts was serving a potent brew, gulped heartily by parishioners who earlier partook in a solemn celebration of the Eucharistic Mass.

The arriving musicians were unhurriedly sorting their seating positions, some with craggy faces beneath felt hats sitting rakishly atop their heads. The cuatro player and fiddler began tuning their instruments in the yard outside Donald Alcide's home. A hammock, clotheslines, a child's swing and a sturdy table and benches set to one side for the party were indications of active outdoor living in the cooler ambient space of the large yard.

The toddlers were first on the scene joined by teenagers after the band played the first recognizable melody. The party hosts were still engaged in a frenzy of preparation over coal pot fires stirring, laying out food and putting last minute touches to the setting. The Hillside compound of Alcide-Pascal family was getting a festive look and a magnet attraction for a limbo district.

Limbo districts was a name used by a political entity to imply areas permanently on a list of postponed projects that had suffered deferments and limited attention because of the passivity of untitled dwellers although every five years their services were requested as part of an army of voters.

The women were arriving ahead of the men, those accompanied broke rank and surged ahead profusely greeting others attending. Lorna as co-guest of honor was boxed in by friends who had not seen her over the years. Lately some men were arriving with telltale signs, unsteady gait with shirttails flapping beneath their jackets.

The music had pumped up in rhythm and Lorna was tugged by her brother Donald out to the center for the first dance and a light cheer broke out. It was a wild cheer with hoots and screams when Mama Nita stepped out with her son Hilton on to the dance floor. The dancing area was soon filled with guests dancing away. Some men made solo forays on to the dance area shunning wives and girlfriends and instead engaged in clowning antics showing their prowess was not in need of a partner. The women paid no attention and when no man asked them to dance, they partnered each other on the dance floor without missing a step.

Karen had gone to the family home along with Jonas to collect a long wooden bench for additional seating. She supported one end and Jonas the other. Without warning she dropped her end, screamed and ran ahead into the partying crowd where she grabbed and pulled Lorna by the arm shouting, "come with me, come with me." There was Herman and the seven Provident children getting off Jacko's truck that was parked on the road a few meters below where Karen and Lorna stood. Lorna hopped, clapped her hands and screamed until they saw her. The children ran ahead of their father and Lorna tried her best to hug all seven in one go. Legs, arms, waist and neck were all embraced and the partygoers paused in admiration as Herman with a hug propped up Lorna to keep her from falling under the weight.

The animated gathering of the reunion offered a timely intermission for lunch and reconciliation. It was felt and being expressed that nothing could exceed or add to the joyful feeling of the party.

Herman was thanking Jacko for the transport and invited him to join the party, which he welcomed above any favor. Although Jacko lived in Hillside, his reputation was that of some esoteric leftover from one of the privileged families that fled the Hillside district many years ago. The community showed little tolerance for his promiscuous behavior but he was able to support his philandering lifestyle with an adequate inheritance. His small frame, flamboyant in bright colored shirts randomly selected blossoming maidens with seductive intent. He was soon in an altercation with the Alcide brothers who disapproved of his vulgar actions while dancing with their sister Karen. Perhaps out of self-preservation, he left the party in obvious disgust when confronted by her brothers.

Donald as "Master of Ceremonies" and life of the party requested that the band play a popular tune in mock relevance to the Provident couple as victims of the Tabor City fire and everyone sung loudly the refrain, "*Fire, Fire in their Wire, Wire, Woy-Woy-Woy, Wy-Ah-Yii.*"

Donald slipped away from the crowd of dancing and singing guests to reconnect with a prized entry. Minutes before, a young resident informed Donald he had shown the way to a stranger who wished to see him. A normally tough and unshakable Donald was moved to emotional reaction when he saw it was Victor.

He wrapped his arms around Victor's legs lifting and carrying him to an unspecified spot. He quickly updated Victor and with his astute sense of drama and excitement tinged with intrigue, he set the stage for entry with Victor, arms around each other's neck dancing into the party to the refrain of, "*Fire Fire in their Wire Wire, Woy-Woy-Woy, Wy-Ah-Yii.*"

A screaming party or a party of screams, either way was an apt description of the scene that followed. Father, mother, uncles and aunts, brothers and sisters, family and friends had already reached maximum ecstasy and appeared spent of all means of praise, someone shouted.

"Oh my God, it can't be! Not another surprise?"

A further lengthy intermission after an unplanned and unfettered family reunion had peaked. The function was copying the format of a stage play and the latest scene fell under act three of the day's proceedings. Some patrons were showing signs of impatience and were seeking a resumption of music and dancing.

Victor was showing his mother lots of attention and was relieved to see her in good health but also happy and enjoying herself.

He was answering her questions about his life at Pine Grove residence of Dr. Keswick when he paused, sat upright and asked,

"By the way have you heard the news?"

"What news is that?"

"I was at the hospital yesterday when Miss Iris passed away."

Lorna stood up abruptly and turned to face her seated son, "Which Miss Iris you talking about?"

"Baxter's Yard Miss Iris of course," Victor confirmed.

"You mean she die."

Lorna was breathing heavily and her face had an overloaded look, weighted down for reasons unknown to a baffled Victor who felt a need to clarify further, "Yes and if you don't believe me you can ask Colom, Blackie or Planche they were there too. Why, what's wrong?"

A hysterical Lorna began shouting while looking up to the heavens, "I knew that, I knew that something happen, my family together on this blessed Sunday. I knew something happen." Lorna fell onto her knees, "now everyone can see what was happening, Lord God on high thank you, my family together again."

After conferring briefly with Victor, Donald assessed the cause of the outburst and with arm around Lorna took her for a long walk. She had ingested such deep hatred of Iris that the effect of the news contrarily triggered a welling up of revulsion and hysteria in Lorna.

51

Miss Iris's funeral was held the following day after her death, the same Sunday the festivities were in progress on Hillside. After the funeral church service, Miss Mable, Winnie Winifred, four fellow venders, and six former Baxter's Yard residents gathered around her graveside singing hymns and giving impromptu eulogies. Miss Mable focused on her strong independent streak and penchant for privacy.

"She frustrated many persons who could not get beyond the wall she built around her, however she always praised her God. Throughout her life Iris wanted to create a space filled with acts of virtue so that people could look up to her and to this end she showed contempt for those living on vice."

Miss Winifred chimed in as Miss Mable either paused or ended her contribution.

"Iris always knew to find that glorious space, one as to do away with evil so the good can prosper and live a life of love detached from hate before hearts with sadness can be emptied and filled with happiness."

A burly vendor with an overflowing torso raised her hand in a request to speak. "I want to say this, Iris wasn't no fool, she speak to each body different depend where you belong, and if it wasn't for the fire she would still be here."

"True, what you say is true," another vendor with stern features began, "it making me ask why that night Iris walk in the dew all the way up that hill where the nuns are, looking for shelter when she could have stopped by Miss Winifred."

"Or why not stop by the presbytery and ask the priests to get in touch with Miss Mable," noted the burly vendor, "Because all she ever talk about is Miss Winnie and Ma Baxter as the only people on this earth she could go to if she needed help."

Miss Mable and Winnie Winifred glanced at each other realizing this was fast becoming a session reproaching others for the tragic circumstances that led to Miss Iris contracting pneumonia.

"Exactly what I have been saying; she was so secretive. Do you realize no one knows her last name title and she refuses to tell anybody?" Miss Mable enlightened present company.

"She told me," the fancy dressed vendor blurted out and all heads turned her way. "I promised her not to tell anyone."

"You know you does lie a lot, how is only you she tell," the burly vendor was using accusatory psychology.

"I don't lie more than you. No one ever find me guilty in court."

"No one ever give me licks for going after their man if you want to know."

Miss Mable and Winnie Winifred began a move away from the gravesite in obvious disgust at the trend of proceedings.

The best dressed followed close behind and caught up with them, "I'm not lying. She did tell me the name bringing her bad luck because her father told her he chose the name because everything that going to happen already waiting to happen and you cannot change it."

Miss Winifred was not impressed. "That's nonsense. Everything is in God's hands and so we cannot know our destiny."

"That's it Iris Destiny, how did you know?"

52

Claire Beaufrand and Lynette Baxter had completed a year in the final class at the convent after having acquired all prospective educational tutoring available for girls. The pair discreetly accepted employment reserved for children of families from an upper social standing and chose to join the staff of the Nation Bank, which offered the highest salaries and status for persons joining the workforce for the first time.

A profile of the convent graduate was a blend of a calm, modest and immaculate young woman entering the protective slipstream of reserved employment as a bank clerk, schoolteacher or civil servant. Moving out of their parents' homes was an option seldom explored as such independent action was thought to be motivated by a desire for concealment. They seldom journeyed off island and were not expected to pursue higher education or acquire a profession but to follow an approved role of awaiting a request of marriage and fulfill their unique responsibility of motherhood.

The young men graduating from St. Teresa's College gave vent to every facet of manhood at every opportunity like victims after prohibition obtaining freedom from former captors. They were given priority over women for the best jobs and justified this claim as being future breadwinners of a family.

The numbers of young men who would be considered counterparts of young women in age and background had dwindled. Many young women remaining in the household were given a debutante's twenty-first birthday party and used the occasion to sometimes declare formally the preferred 'boyfriend' at the cake-cutting event.

During midday lunch breaks while employed with the bank, Claire and Lynette were working to reestablish the sociable relationship that existed between them as students at the convent. Available time for sociable activity had been greatly reduced because of work demands. It was even more limited because they lived on opposite sides of the fire ravaged Tabor city. The fire also burnt out former midpoint meeting places such as the cinemas and ice cream parlors that were popular hives of congregating youth.

Claire and Lynette sat together in the bank's cafeteria having a light lunch. "No word yet if the ship has arrived?" inquired Lynette casually.

"Maybe in a day or two," guessed Claire.

"Have you come across Victor lately?" a concerned Lynette asks Claire.

"You know he lives at Dr. Keswick's home not too far from us, "

"Yes, he called to thank me soon after he was freed, Dr. Keswick must have told him it was me who first informed him of the arrest," Lynette had made Claire aware of this several times before.

"I saw him just yesterday at a little shop in the neighborhood."

"Really, what did he say?"

"He was buying a newspaper and said Dr. Keswick was waiting for it, so we didn't have much time to talk."

"I am not saying this because he is the only one in our gang still here but Victor is the most helpful, fun-loving and well-mannered of all, successfully graduating educationally and socially in all departments with honors," boasted Lynette. "You would believe it would be the other way around compared to the others."

"It is a pity you can only praise and appreciate him up to a point," Claire cautioned.

"What point? Just like you to always leave your thoughts hanging."

Claire laughed, 'Yes, but the noose is not going to be around my neck."

"There you go again. Why are you being sarcastic?"

"You are making deep pronouncements and I am being helpful so you don't get hurt."

"Me! Deep? Hurt? I just made a simple comment about a nice guy and mutual friend, what's got into you?"

Claire did not respond, but Lynette was determined to probe for reasons and to bring out her present thoughts.

"Oh, I know why you are acting that way. It is because you are missing Vivian and Tom," teased Lynette still trying to undo Claire's aloof attitude.

"No, no, I am finding the change interesting."

"When you say this, I mean don't you miss them?" Lynette inquired in a cordial tone.

"You grow up and begin to appreciate other people and how things affect them differently." Claire continued to reply vaguely.

"I experienced the same thing when I used to visit with my Aunty Mable before the fire and saw how Victor and his family lived."

"But there is no chance your Aunty Mable will change the way she thinks," Claire said observantly.

"I beg your pardon. Do you know she is the one who paid Victor's school fees at St. Teresa's College? At first, I didn't want to believe it."

"And do you realize it was for Victor's father she did it?"

"So what does it matter? She knew Victor was the one who would be going to school."

"It matters if she had other motives which means she has not really changed."

The midday hour was naturally the busiest in the cafeteria and male staff in particular was constantly interrupting their conversation with complimentary remarks directed at Claire and only periodic greetings offered to Lynette.

"I have lost track, we were reflecting on how we feel about our friends and I said Victor stood out and that seemed to irritate you."

Claire laughed and shook her head but it was Lynette, who persisted, "Maybe you think he is not good enough for me," Lynette said regretfully. An ominous sign the symbiosis of their relationship was threatened.

"Is that what's on your mind and are you trying to make me think like you? Well you're wrong because if he is good enough for me I suppose he would be good enough for you too."

Lynette's face twitched in frustration and shock. "I hope you can explain your actions to Vivian or is it Tom or is it whoever."

Claire sprung off her chair and spoke in French pronouncing her words with emphasis to ensure their significance whether understood or not.

"Un oiseau dans la main vaut deux tu l'auras," Claire said, quickly walking away.

Lynette sat alone quietly for a while ruminating over their best-friend days. Claire was an expert at making statements that could have so many meanings, she thought to herself.

It was unimaginable to Lynette that Claire's attitude would have changed so radically because signs of a rift in their friendship on leaving school were never apparent. One quick analysis after another could not pinpoint why a happy and vibrant gang that had been disbanded by a severe fire and departure for study overseas had not as expected drawn the two of them even closer together.

Lynette sat alone with a minute left before resuming the afternoon shift of work. "Call Victor," "Call Victor," "Call Victor" repeated like a voice alarm in her head.

Lynette called a third time on the phone and finally was able to talk to him.

"Where have you been?

"I rang several times and they said you were not there."

"Can I see you sometime soon? I need to talk with you about something."

"Yes, is it important?"

"I will tell you what it is when I see you."

"How about lunchtime tomorrow?"

"You can meet me at the bank and I will buy you lunch."

"I wish I could have prevented the fire from destroying all the eating places."

"What is wrong with the bank cafeteria? It is about the only decent place since the fire."

"Since when have you become concerned about my reputation?"

"I don't care, you were never in the picture before. It was all Vivian and Tom, so why should you worry now about what she's thinking?"

"Just find yourself there tomorrow, okay?"

53

Seventeen year-old Sophie, the eldest daughter, cried constantly during and after the family reunion. This attracted the comforting attention of Karen who was Lorna's youngest sister and mother of a twin boy and girl of two years.

A concerned Karen hoped to get to the reason for Sophie's distress with a new approach.

"Sophie, come here. I have a surprise for you," Karen said enticingly.

"What's it?" Sophie asked momentarily enthused and hastened to beside the ironing table.

Karen was ironing a pleated skirt, which she lifted off the table to show her. "How do you like it?" Karen asked.

"Remember I told you it was a nice style and it fits you well." Sophie said openly.

"This is not the same one, since you liked mine I did this one especially for you, I went and bought some more material."

"But, but," a surprised Sophie started, then paused, "but you didn't even measure me."

Karen grinned. "I got a skirt from your clothes and made it the same size so it should be the right fit."

Sophie looked at Karen with an awkward stare and said nothing. Karen unhappy with the silence added, "You see how clever I am, I wanted to surprise you that is why I did not measure you. Come on try it on to see."

Sophie declined with a shake of her head and continued with doleful eyes to look detached. Karen decided on a direct approach to unearth what was the matter, "Tell me. I am trying everything to make you happy, but all my efforts are being rejected by you."

Sophie's reaction was more than a surprise. "Why didn't you ask me if I wanted a skirt? I do not want it and I not going to wear it. Furthermore, leave me alone."

Karen stood still for a good few minutes after Sophie had walked away. Soon after she decided to immediately go in search of Lorna to discuss Sophie's evident problem. Sophie went to Jonas for directions on the quickest way to reach Lorna.

"Follow that road," Jonas pointed to a narrow grass covered track, "cause where it is, is not far from here and walk until you reach an old broken down house just over there."

Sophie walked for two miles before she saw the derelict building half a mile away. Herman and Lorna were inspecting the property in close consultation with Donald who was enticing Herman with a variety of incentives to settle and live in the Hillside district and develop a partnership.

Donald claimed he held the deed of sale for the dilapidated property. Its outer shutters dangle and sway on one hinge and the unlocked doors slammed with every gust of wind. Roof-level breezes whistled beneath loose clattering zinc sheets on which flocks of blackbirds were aggressively prancing and chirping.

Stepping inside the building, the ghost-like atmosphere faded away and noises softened in the brightly painted interior. There were no ghost marks or signs of cobweb.

"I paid a very small amount for this property" Donald boasted. "The reason is because it had a bad name for being haunted. Of course I quickly got rid of those so-called ghosts but only after the ghosts chased away the lazy vagabonds who don't want to work."

No one had attached significance to Karen's arrival or made reference to her presence until Donald threw her into the incentives mix without her approval.

"Look who's arrived! Another good reason to stay here. Karen can help you with looking after the children and you can have more time for yourself."

"I always hear people say when they agree, 'I second the motion.'" Lorna's tone was in the upper range of enthusiasm.

"I will have to think about it," Karen said calmly as they began their walk back to the family home. At this juncture Karen was reluctant to introduce a new family crisis that would deprive Lorna of a well-deserved period of blissful and contented feeling having just overcome moods of desolation and misery.

Lorna unexpectedly confirmed her feelings of contentment as she danced a pirouette and explained, "I don't know how to tell you all about how I am feeling. I don't know if it is because I am on a hill high above with all family, those I am born with and those that I am married to."

"And like you did, the young ones will grow up and leave home with their own family." Karen added.

"You know I don't mind that especially how I see Victor handle himself. He do good at school, have high-up friends and I waiting to see something when it comes to his girlfriends," Lorna raised her eyebrows apprehensively at the end of the statement.

"Well after that it's Sophie next in line," Karen said carefully, testing for Lorna's reaction.

"Eh, eh, Sophie not in that. She have a little time to go before but Johnny right behind."

"So why Sophie and the other girl-children not going to get the same chance?" Karen asked.

"But what get into you Karen? See if the Baxter girl and the French people daughter not here still, they join the bank until husband come around for dem to make the children."

Karen became increasingly nervous, aware disclosure could wipe out current feelings of euphoria. Unavoidably and always regrettably the next major concern was on its way to cast a dark shadow in a mind chamber now aglow with pride.

"So are you going to look for a husband for Sophie?"

"Don't rush my child. When she ready and well knows herself and—." Lorna was interrupted by her son Johnny who apparently gave her a message and caused her to hurry ahead of everyone.

"Hello-o-o Virginia, my old friend."

They had arrived at Donald's home where a friend awaited Lorna.

"Where have you been since the fire?" an ebullient Lorna hugged Virginia.

"That fire, it really wicked you know, it force people to move all over the place. In every part of Au Tabor they have people from Baxter's Yard and now I will have to search for my friends where they are," announced Virginia expressing concern.

"You can say that again," Lorna affirmed.

"So what is the latest news, where I am I don't hear anything."

"Well nothing much since Miss Iris died," Virginia suddenly gave a loud gasp.

"Oh no, may her soul rest in peace; when that happen?"

"She dead and buried already since last Sunday," assured

Lorna.

"I tell you where I am nobody tell me anything, all I am hearing is gossip about who friendly with who, and this one making baby for so and so but the things that matter most they don't tell me."

54

Karen returned to the maternal home and made no attempt to reconnect with Sophie until she noticed her packing her clothes and personal items together. Sophie saw Karen looking on and did not wait for a question, "I am going to stay with my mother," she said evenly.

Karen refrained from asking any questions, knowing it would only cause additional protest and dispute. She did, however, try for positive communication.

"Do you need help with anything?" Karen asked hopefully.

"If I need, I will ask," Sophie replied curtly.

"Hello Sophie, remember me?" Virginia asked gratuitously as Sophie joined her surprised mother and acted quickly in response.

"Of course, I do. Excuse me while I go and rest these things inside," Sophie said, hurriedly carrying a bundle of her clothes.

Lorna did not want a possible dispute to be aired in the presence of Virginia and so was constrained to request a reason immediately for Sophie's sudden appearance. But the concerned look on Lorna's face nudged Virginia to ask, "What? Is something wrong? You look worried."

"She has not been feeling well of late and on her face you can see she's not well."

Just then, Sophie reappeared, apparently just to offer an excuse, "I didn't know you had someone with you. I will be taking a rest until you finish." Then she turned and left before anyone could get another word out.

"You not telling me, but I see for myself." The statement by Virginia lingered for a while.

"See what?" a distracted Lorna asked.

"I thought my eyes told me Sophie going to have a baby."

A disbelieving Lorna reacted with a displeased wave of the hand and looked confused and uncertain, then muttered disconnectedly,

"Why do you want to say things like that and what makes you think so? I wonder; do you want me to tell Herman what you said?"

Lorna in an instinctive moment wanted Virginia to leave immediately to avoid further discomfort, but she composed herself and called for Herman as her first line of support.

Virginia began to sense her own discomfort in a situation she had casually brought to light. She stood up to say goodbye aware the issue had severely disrupted normal discourse and bodily function. Lorna's body slumped in her chair and she was oblivious of her friend's presence, understandably preoccupied with the revelation.

Lorna irrationally believed all her problems were entombed with Miss Iris. Her mind was unreceptive and in disbelief. Sophie's distended waistline had nothing to do with child bearing. Surprisingly Lorna implored Virginia to remain.

She called out to Herman again but this time added a sound of urgency.

"Herman, please come right now! Please, please!"

She no longer doubted Virginia's observation was correct after recalling various indications from her sister Karen about Sophie's condition.

Herman strolled into view with a contrasting calm.

"Go ahead, tell him what you notice," Lorna instructed Virginia having disqualified herself.

Virginia looked at Lorna in amazement and paused.

Having heard her mother calling, Sophie just then returned to the room, concerned about whatever was going on.

"Unfold your arms Sophie," Lorna said to Sophie harshly.

Sophie kept her arms folded over her stomach, then turned around and marched away angrily.

"What's going on here? What is all this about?" Herman was suddenly aware that something odd was happening.

"Your Sophie is expecting a baby," Lorna announced boldly with assured stance and hands on her hips. Herman looked uncertain and stared impassively at the two women. He was not sure why they wanted to rely on him for an answer to a problem that mainly concerned women. As far as he knew, pregnancy was a woman's business in which men played no further part. Whenever Lorna was pregnant she consulted with other women and only casually mentioned it when he made advances to her.

Five years ago Karen was in the same position, maybe a little older and had twins. He noticed how Mama Nita doted over them, which made him believe they would be able to help, so Herman called a young nephew standing nearby.

"Alan, run and tell Karen I want to see her. Tell her to hurry, eh."

Herman was sneaking away from present company when Lorna warned,

"Don't go far, you will have to talk to Sophia about her plans because I don't know who up here can deliver babies."

"I already send for Karen," Herman assured Lorna.

55

Victor entered the bank to keep the date Lynette had adamantly requested on the phone and attracted to the service counter four female staffers. Lynette did not join them, but in a jealous ploy kept her head lowered.

"Hi Lynette, whenever you're ready." As Victor indicated the purpose of his visit, the four ladies began peeling away from the counter.

Claire Beaufrand was notably absent during this lunchtime hour. Customarily she would inform Lynette of any planned absence and in most cases advised of her intended whereabouts.

"Victor, I find it very strange Claire went somewhere and never told me," revealed Lynette as they sat down to have a meal.

"Sometimes people have a little change of mood and act differently," suggested Victor.

"Un huh, making excuses for her. Have you noticed any change with me and my mood?"

Victor paused to swallow a mouthful of food. "I will tell you what the difference is. She is freer to go and come and be friends with whom she pleases."

"So can I. Don't forget I am now a working person."

"So then why don't you act like one?" Victor challenged back.

"Even though I did Victor, you make it so difficult just to see you. Are you trying to distance yourself from me and if so, why?"

"Don't blame me for what the fire has caused, you don't have your aunt's house in town anymore and it is now like a desert between where we live. Tell me, when or where you tried to see me?"

"It is more than that, your attitude is different, you no longer care to see me like you did before."

"If I had been on my way to England then you would not have had to complain and accuse me unfairly."

"Alright from now on you will notice the difference, I will be choosing to see who I want to see, when I want, make my own arrangements and I will not let anyone stop me."

"Yes, but those persons who they don't approve of will still feel uncomfortable even though you insist on seeing them."

"See what I mean? Every time I try to remove all the difficulties, you keep bringing up new ones."

"These aren't new concerns. The fact is, any effort to restrict you from being in the company of someone is bound to have an effect on them."

"Victor when you refer to those persons, do you mean it to include yourself?"

"Of course, am I not among the lesser ones?"

"In the community I knew around Baxter's Yard, the Provident family was well respected and I can say I never heard Aunty Mae say one bad thing about you."

"Good or bad, I wish she had said something about me so I would know where I stood in her eyes."

"Okay, forgetting all what Aunty Mae has done for you and your family, let us change the subject. Tell me what it is between you and

Claire?" An assertive Lynette tried a direct strategy.

"I really don't understand the question because you know us both very well and we all have been friends for a long while."

"What I notice, if I just mention your name, she makes some very critical and negative remarks about me as if I have no right to say anything concerning you."

"Oh boy, I am not going to get involved in any quarrel between the two of you, it just happened that I live not far from Claire. The Keswicks and the Beaufrands are good friends and visit each other. I can go to Claire's home and she can visit me anytime."

"And before all that happened, who took you from where you were at an early age and made you what you are today."

"Even your aunty will agree God made me and who I am today depended on how I used the opportunities before me. C'mon, pull yourself together cause I am running out of patience. Comments like that is what –" Victor appeared to have lost his appetite. He pushed the rest of his food aside and ceased to eat.

"Obviously you do not mind being used now that Vivian and Tom are not around." Lynette's face was aglow with confidence that his smug defense had weakened.

"Getting to know someone takes time and opportunity. Without competition, Claire and I have got much closer, we have a clearer understanding of each other's feelings," Victor acknowledged, choosing a calm and forthright strategy.

Lynette went silent and lowered her eyes. "You took long to admit it," she muttered weakly after a long pause. She was surprised by the openness.

"Admit what?" his tone edgy and terse.

Lynette was silent again, the harsh pointed question stabbed at her heart. She may have been choking down tears or genuinely needed some air.

"I am going for a walk," she said rising from her seat.

"A walk? Your lunch break is nearly over," Victor said with concern.

Lynette did not answer or say goodbye. She walked quickly out the door.

56

The sea had lost its blue-green tint and now mirrored the dull grey of an overcast sky. Chill winds gusted without a pause on day seven and the four students' memories of Au Tabor receded with the changing atmospheric conditions. Thoughts and minds focused on the approaching new domicile two sailing days away.

Preliminary thoughts and resolutions were finding expression among the students revealing certain anxiety of life in England.

"I wonder if I can get a part-time job I want to send a passage for my girlfriend to come up," Martin moaned for most of the journey over his girlfriend.

"Man you ever hear about the saying bringing coals to Newcastle, or back home we say 'bringing sand to the beach,' the amount of girls up here," Tom said with caution.

"I hear they cold and snobbish. All I want is get my degree and head back home," Vivian chimed in. "Although I am supposed to look up so many family member living all over England."

"I hope you all will be in the congregation to hear my powerful sermons that will move all of you closer to becoming good Christians."

Tom had exempted himself from future prayer before meals sessions underscoring his disregard for Zane's latest theocratic posturing.

"It's okay, Tom. My faith teaches everyone has a free will and can either choose to accept the word of God or decide on his own path to hell and damnation."

"Sounds more like a threat than a choice of free will," Tom noted. "Can I have goodwill instead and hopefully you will not use prayer to make fun of me."

"Tom has a point," Vivian in unusual support of Tom made the others attentive. "A free will which is of equivocal design, yet has clearly stated limitations within which free will is either rewarded or punished, should refrain from using the term free and refer it rather as a choice of good or bad expressions of will. Conversely I am not aware if the term 'free will' was meant to be idiomatic."

Zane and Martin looked at each other in a mock show of failure to understand Vivian's argument.

"The man hasn't even reached a university and already big words flying over my head much less after he graduate," Martin said with a raw Au Tabor accent.

Details of arrival and disembarkation were being announced over the intercom and interrupted conversation.

"A new life, a new existence away from loved ones." Martin said with surprisingly cautious introspection.

The following morning, four eager students were on the ship's deck at first light viewing the skyline of London. They now seemed inseparable coordinating preparation and timing their movements with each other.

They were met by a representative of the West Indian High Commission who guided them through immigration and customs procedures. They would be staying at a student's hostel run by the Commission until further boarding arrangements were concluded for their respective places of study.

206

The first order of business was to extract every bit of news available on the aftermath of the fire. Victor's misadventure with the police drew the indignation of the four students who closed ranks without exception promising to send a formal protest copied to as many in authority as possible. Assuming with some certainty their presence on the island would have averted such an incident, a sense of estrangement overcame them as missing voices of influence.

57

Herman was not nearby when Karen showed up and asked Lorna abruptly, "Where's Herman?"

"He's somewhere around."

"He send to call me. Do you know for what?" Karen wanted to ensure the reason for her presence was understood.

"Pass behind the house to see if you find him," Lorna suggested.

When Karen left, Lorna turned to Virginia. "I never see a man like that always giving somebody else his business to do for him."

Karen returned alone. "I haven't seen him. You sure you all don't know why he want to see me. Alan told me he was talking to you all."

"I suppose he want to give you the news that Sophie is going to have a baby."

"Oh! I am not surprised."

"So why you not surprised? You mean all that time you knew?"

"But all that time I was trying to tell you but you did act as if I was interfering in your family business."

"Karen, you mean if you come and tell me something that happen to my family, I will get vex? After all." Lorna said slowly, querying Karen's apparent mistrust.

"To be honest, if I was very sure how you would take it, I would have told you."

Any chance of an escalating dispute was thwarted by Herman's sudden reappearance with questions that confounded the three women.

"So what have you all decided?" asked Herman.

The ladies looked around inquiringly and at each other for an answer that came after an embarrassing pause. "We decided you should find out who the somebody is who got your daughter pregnant and let us know if he has an explanation," said Virginia, a comment she thought would reveal the culprit and not be resented.

"Has she said who it is?"

The three women stared at Herman in dismay.

"She's in the bedroom upstairs. Go and ask her." Lorna crossed her legs and changed her seated direction in a show of disgust.

"Herman is no help. On the other hand Lorna, have you, as a mother, sat with her and listened to what she has to say?"

Virginia saw this as opportunity to make an exit from the midst of a sensitive family issue. After the break for goodbyes, Karen brought Lorna up to date on her contact with Sophie regarding the skirt and her latest wish to be with her mother. Lorna was visibly moved, tears running down her cheeks. Karen declined her request to be with her while she sat with Sophie.

"She needs you, you and you." This was the extent to which Karen could explain emphatically how she perceived Sophie's need for her mother.

"Herman, come here," Lorna said, springing into action. "I want you to tell Victor about Sophie because she will have to see the doctor and maybe he could arrange for him to see her. You know I met Dr. Keswick and we had a nice chat."

The tables had turned and now Lorna had the connections to make things happen. She got off her chair on the patio and waved a final hello of the afternoon to some persons on the public access path a short distance away.

After entering the house she lumbered up the stairway and before reaching the bedroom could be heard cautiously asking, "Sophie, darling, are you awake?"

58

Getting a message to his son, Victor, proved an intricate problem for Herman. Before Tabor City was reduced to an ashen wasteland, someone could obtain random assistance and seek nondescript information at popular places of assembly. Persons at Herman's social and economic level needing help or guidance regularly intercepted anyone who outwardly appeared competent in that respect.

Citizens adhered to that particular layered orderliness of the society where few risked living above their means or pretended knowledge and intellect above their recognized educational training and exposure. Anyone noticed posing socially beyond their public status and did not 'know-their-place' risked being ridiculed and, in some cases, ostracized.

In the past, Miss Mable would have allowed him to use her telephone or convey a message on his behalf. This directed his mind to her nearest relation available remembering her niece Lynette was working at the bank and was part of a group of friends with whom Victor kept company.

"Hello, Mr. Provident, how can I help?" Lynette quickly approached the counter with a personal touch no other clerk could claim.

"How did you know you are the one I wanted to see?" Herman

asked suspiciously. He started looking around, intimidated by the staid and ordered appearance of the bank's interior. His income level did not meet the bank's minimum deposit to have an account or transact business and it was the first time he had entered the premises.

"What happened? Is there something wrong?" Lynette asked, quickly ignoring his first concern.

"Oh, I want to know if you can do me a favor."

"Sure, what is it?" Lynette asked brightly.

"I want you to tell Victor for me that I would like to see him as soon as he can."

Lynette's anxiety was partly relieved when she heard this.

"Is that all?"

"Well, yes, for the time being."

"Okay, then wait here. I will try right away."

"Thank you, Miss. Miss Mable raise you just like herself, always ready to help."

Lynette returned to the counter sooner than expected. "No one is answering the phone," she said. "I will try later or maybe I can give him the message for you when I get him."

Lynette attempted to extract the message and sensed it was probably important based on the extraordinary effort Herman had made to contact Victor. Regardless of her spat with Victor the day before, she felt an attachment to the Provident family and recalled Victor's expressed feelings of appreciation for her efforts to seek his release following his arrest. She had not reproached him or regretted her part in spite of his recent disregard of her.

"The message is really for him to give to Dr. Keswick," Herman explained as he watched Lynette's sudden surprise. When he realized her jaw remained open and she was looking past him, he spun around and saw Victor approaching from the bank entrance.

THE PROVIDENT FAMILY OF BAXTERS YARD

"Are you appealing to my father? Well, I am here to make my apology in person," Victor joked. "Or is he using you as a courier to get a message to your Aunty Mable?"

Herman was convinced Lynette and Victor were in some conspiracy evidenced by the prompt responses to his mission request.

Victor was right away made aware of the actual situation by Lynette and directed proceedings from then on.

"Daddy, have a seat over there, I will be with you in a minute." He then beckoned Lynette to come closer and leaned over the customer side of the counter.

"I am serious about an apology." Then, in a soft voice while handing her a bag of plums, he added, "You deserve to be treated with more respect than I have shown you. I picked these for you."

Lynette accepted the parcel and with a suspicious stare. "Thank you. Do I have to share these with Claire? Oh, I forgot you didn't have to bring hers to the bank, she's just next door."

Victor seemed unhappy with the remark, but Lynette did not pause.

"Go find out what your father wants," she advised. "He looks worried."

"My father, the real Mr. Provident is okay. What he worries about is the Herman Provident he wishes to see in the mirror."

"Well, I don't know, but he says he wants you to give Dr. Keswick a message for him."

Mention of the doctor seemed to make Victor move to find out without further delay the reason his father requested this meeting. In spite of his father's protestation that he would rather talk outside, Victor sat with him in the bank's customer waiting section. Herman felt he was not an equal in these surroundings and secretly wanted to remind Victor of his prior misadventure.

Herman had knowledge that the social template based on a gradation of color and class nullified his son's chance of getting a job at the bank. One need not apply if you are not from the middle to upper echelons of society. This carried an inference that those born of indigent families were not trustworthy irrespective of competence. The ambiguity was heightened when for unfounded reasons light skin color was given a higher rating than competence in the selection of applicants.

This setting designed to store secrets and safeguard large amounts of money made Herman nervous he could be a victim of unwarranted suspicion since others might not be aware of the reason for his presence.

Lately Victor had developed immunity to the opinion of others, toughened after his episode with the police and maintained a present temperament that did not permit intimidation.

59

The news of Sophie's pregnancy disheartened Victor. He had had a secret wish, a hope, that Sophie would emulate Claire and Lynette, and adopt similar basic principles and codes of behavior. They would not have children until they were married. Why did Sophie not wait until she got a husband, he asked? It would have been a good example to set.

In fulfillment of his longing, he often portrayed himself as a prime example of how aspiring to a higher standard contrary to those observed in the former Baxter's Yard environment could have benefitted and achieved for her a better future. He maintained his boast even when facing ridicule over his arrest and pointed to the fact that his social connections combined with an aggressive stance of his innocence drew public attention to his case.

Victor's actions and relationships were a pantomime of his parent's combined qualities and configured his decision-making. On many occasions he invited Sophie to spend daytime hours with him for her to experience and be infused with the content of discussions, information and activities of his friends.

Despite Mrs. Keswick's approval, he blocked a request for Sophie to share the spacious liveried quarters at the Keswick home. He lamely alluded to her lack of an education level necessary to fit into this setting, which he said could be an embarrassment if she did not have the appropriate level of communication and comportment. He however steered clear of accepting blame for Sophie's crisis and reclined upright from his bent over posture after a long silence.

"Who is the bastard responsible for this?" Victor asked his father.

Herman was unaccustomed to such harsh language, especially from his son.

"What do you mean?" Herman asked.

"Somebody had to get her pregnant. Who it is?"

"She will not say even though her mother keeps asking her over and over."

"Okay, I will ask her myself."

"She will say is only when she go to confession, if the priest ask her for the name that she will give him for the child to baptize."

Not surprisingly children born into families with the mother as the single parent comprised a majority in several small communities. However the children received communal love, support and protection until adulthood but needed to make a giant step if hoped to join the mainstream of social and economic life in the towns.

"You said you have a message for Dr. Keswick?"

"Your mother is the one who mentioned if you can arrange for Dr. Keswick to see Sophie."

"Dr. Keswick is a surgeon and does not deliver babies. Why doesn't she call Nurse Grace who delivered nearly all the children in Baxter's Yard?" summarily dismissing his father and, with it, his undertaking to obtain the services of Dr. Keswick.

Herman hastened his goodbyes, pointing to the bad weather for his hurried departure. He looked despondent recalling a persistent failing of his initiative to forge a notable image of his family.

The road to Hilltop twisted up the hillside and was twice the distance of the almost perpendicular footpath access. Herman struggled up the muddy path, sliding and forced frequently to lend his hands to propel himself upward.

Although wet and obviously tired, Lorna hounded Herman for report on his mission. She was elated that he had met with Victor, but she was disappointed.

"You know something told me I should have gone myself especially if I knew I would meet Victor." Her body language said it all. He had failed again.

"Anyway, Sophie said she went to confession and confessed everything to the priest. Of course you know he cannot tell what he hears in confession, but she said Father Lambert told her it was not a sin if she refused to name the father."

"If she can tell Father Lambert, why she cannot tell me, her real father?" Herman said in a rare assertive display.

"Have you asked her, don't just say so?" Lorna felt he didn't mean what he said.

"You said she already made up her mind to only tell the priest," Herman passed off the challenge.

"Is a miracle you ain't arranging yet to see Ma Baxter," Lorna said with scorn.

60

Jonas Alcide was referred to sometimes among family and friends as the bushman. His regular and solo disappearances into the dense foliage of the mountains as though in collaboration with some intermediary resident of the hillside lent to his reputation as a mystic. He provisioned the entire extended family and was an important supplier to the food market of the district.

Jonas showed signs of asceticism from an early age and was only fourteen years old when he stoutly defended a large tree his parents were planning to cut down to allow extension of their living quarters. He ignored threats of punishment for being rebellious and protested.

"This tree is living longer than any man who was ever born on this earth," he had said then. "Trees bear fruit to keep us alive while all we do is to eat what the tree sends. We use it to build house and make all kinds of furniture. You see us living here now, if the tree was not there before, the land we stand on now would have washed away already."

He had threatened to leave for good if they cut the tree down. And when they did, he disappeared to a nearby forest for a week. When he returned, bedraggled and calm, he had remained unrepentant over his absence.

Following that episode, he continued to visit the forest alone to live off the land and enjoy nature and extracted its surpluses for the nearby communities.

The children were excitedly accepting plums and mangoes from Uncle Jonas brought from the forest when little Johnny Provident reminded.

"Uncle Jonas, when you goin to take us to the river again by where you have the pigs?"

"You have a good memory," Jonas said, sounding impressed. "But do you remember how far it is and how you cried and we had to carry you because you got tired?"

"Now I am a big boy. I won't get tired this time," Johnny said, proudly defending himself.

"Okay, okay, we'll see. Remember you are a town boy."

Jonas made the comparison with Johnny's Hillside cousins in mind who, because of the lifestyle and terrain, were more physically fit.

Jonas discussed Johnny's request with family members and it was agreed to have a family picnic next to the river, which was a two-hour walk along a narrow track through the forest.

61

Preparations were in progress for the planned riverside picnic. There was an ominous calm in the air. Wind vanes were at a standstill, and indications of an area of low pressure were confirmed by a light but steady breeze blowing opposite to the usual northeasterly flow. The air was filled with lots of winged insects floating about in clusters, a familiar indication of approaching inclement weather. Later in the evening, the insects in countless numbers swarmed around the lamplight and before long fell lifeless in some collective rite of passage to another firmament.

Sitting with the family making last minute plans for the following day's picnic, the bushman in Jonas looked up at the skyline and sniffed the air. He observed bands of dark clouds curling up the eastern sky, and he sighed deeply because he could not bear the thought of cancelling the picnic and disappointing the children. He was known for creating imaginary forest adventures for them with his storytelling. It stirred in them a genuine interest to experience those fantasies.

It also dawned on Jonas that the stories were based on his own intuitive thoughts and that he had inadvertently employed the young ones to understand his own convictions.

His desire to relate his love and respect for all creatures living in the forest was inspired by the wide-eyed stares of the children, attentive and trusting, as he sought to make those stories interesting and plausible in an idyllic setting of the forest.

Having spent much of his life in the pristine environment of the forest Jonas did not participate in religious activity. He purposefully disregarded church doctrines designed to curb natural gifts and pleasures of mind and body and considered normal emotions of the human spirit should not be given up to self-denial. His natural state of existence was in conflict with ritual claiming to ordain man to a higher being beyond his innate abilities. He prided himself for not engaging in the worship of a secular imagery on a planet already possessed with infinite works of perfection, all original, innovative and beyond imitation or replication by man. However innate his knowledge, he could not predict the moment in time the storm would impact.

62

The din of rain showers overhead on the zinc-covered roof was not always an intrusive noise. Many individuals related to the sounds as soothing, comforting and embracing, it was welcomed when shutting out other disturbance and insulated a mind in a studio effect and permitted the arousal of esoteric thoughts.

A warning of expected bad weather created a protective frame of mind in Lorna and she was persuaded to collect all her offsprings, mother-hen style under her wing. She was entering a defensive phase relating Sophie's pregnancy to a misfortune that could have been avoided had there been adequate supervision. Her family was now all together and some were no longer staying at her parent's family a mile away.

The families were shut in their respective houses within the compounds all day and for the first time unable to mingle because of the persistent deluge and consequent flooding of the ground.

In the Mama Nita family, Karen sent the children of the household off to sleep happily. "C'mon go to bed if you all don't want to miss the picnic. I am sure your cousins are already sleeping."

Without hesitation they all skipped off to their beds. Jonas marveled at the invincibility of youth never for a moment considering the rain or perhaps any force of nature could be a hindrance.

The children slept and did not stir as the house shook after each blast of thunder roared out of the sky. Karen and Mama Nita hastened to cover every mirror and reflective surface with bed-sheets reacting to bright flashes of lightning that made quick circuits around rooms of the house.

Karen then warned Jonas, "I hope you know I am not letting you take the children anywhere in this weather."

Ironically, Jonas was considered the impulsive one in the family. He was known for adventurous exploits and could expose them to danger. He laid awake all night, immobilized with fearful thoughts an imminent disaster might come to pass. The rain showers had not ceased. He had never experienced such a sustained rainstorm and wondered if the mountain was being weakened by the continual showers.

Closer to dawn, a thud, a rumble of crashing sounds shook the mountain and there was simultaneous opening of bedroom doors and acts of swift motion indicating panic and urgency by occupants of the household. Jonas rushed to the closed front door and on opening checked his vision, blinking several times to ensure he was not having distorted vision. A large slab of the hillside's green facade had slid to the bottom and left a giant gash exposing the mountain's pith of brown soil. Jonas gave out a cavernous roar as he became aware the house occupied by the Provident family was located on the slab and had plummeted down the hill.

Amid screams, Jonas made his way down the footpath adjacent to the landslide where the scene was soon teeming with members of the district. Within the hour, medical personnel and an ambulance had arrived on the scene and became the obvious authority in the rescue effort and triage process. Soon the first rescue of a surviving casualty was brought from among the debris by Jonas. He carried the unconscious body of Sophie Provident. When it was realized she had a pulse and was pregnant, she was immediately whisked off to hospital by ambulance accompanied by Jonas.

It was overcast with a light drizzle and occasional thunder could still be heard in the distance. Swirling muddy water on the road made travelling slow and hazardous. Jonas sat in the back of the ambulance unable to maintain his composure, shaking his head continuously as if trying to shake off a bad dream.

Victor had travelled to the hospital with Dr. Keswick who was urgently summoned to duty because of anticipated casualties from the landslide and storm.

On arrival at the hospital, Jonas observed the attendants removing Sophie from the ambulance and he heard someone in an anxious voice ask the ambulance driver, "Are you from by where they had the landslide?"

"Yes, man. Is a bad situation and plenty confusion"

"Can I get a lift with you? My family lives around there."

When Jonas realized Victor was the person asking for the ride, he called out loudly to him, "Victor," and called out a second time to get his attention, "Victor, its me, Uncle Jonas," then quickly walked up to a startled Victor and wrapped both arms around him, lifted him off his feet and walked away with a wrestling Victor in his arms.

"What happen, what happen, why you holding me like that?" an alarmed Victor demanded.

Jonas had to wrestle many animals into compliance and realized the importance of gaining physical submission as he delivered the painful and injurious news, horrific and devastating in scale.

"Bad news, very bad news, I only got Sophie so far," Jonas blurted out.

"I don't understand what you telling me"

Jonas said in a tremulous voice, "The whole hill come down."

"Which hill, which hill?" Victor asked with a voice of increasing anxiety.

"The hill bury all the people who were living on it with your family, mother, father, children, everybody."

Jonas's method to restrain and subjugate through physical exertion was not easy as a robust Victor escaped his grasp several times and threatened to join his family by submitting to some form of self-extinction.

It was some two hours later Dr. Keswick got word that people were gathering on the hill next to the hospital curiously observing throes of grief by Victor. The group made room for the doctor to collect Victor and lead him back to the hospital compound. Then Jonas gave the doctor an eyewitness account of the disaster.

Dr. Keswick sat in his office with Jonas and Victor and the renowned surgeon, in command and in control, set about with composure, the task of relaying the news.

"I, too, am exhausted having spent the better part of two hours in the operating room," he said before pausing to examine the faces before him. "But I am happy to report the good news." Dr. Keswick got up and strolled from behind his desk, "Despite being slightly premature I was able to save and deliver a baby girl from the mother, Sophie Provident."

Both Jonas and Victor sat up and turned to the doctor with looks of gratitude for a new life born out of a tragic occurrence. Dr. Keswick stood directly behind a seated Victor and rested a firm hand on each of his shoulders giving the impression he was holding him down. "However, sadly, I was unable to save the mother's life."

63

The daunting series of events surrounding the landslide, culminating in the birthing of a healthy appealing newborn, aroused heartrending sentiment on the island. The tragic tale of the Provident family remained as the headline for many weeks and was reported overseas in many countries. Some people explained away the tragedy of land slippage as an "Act of God," and romanticized the survival of the baby to miracle status. The dreadful annihilation of a family was later referred to as a secondary feature of the tragedy.

Praise for the surgical skills of Dr. Keswick circulated throughout the communities brought into the picture Dora, the doctor's wife, also a social worker who began recruiting a number of fellow socialites to provide for the baby's present and future needs.

The physical aspects and makeup of the newborn was a subject much discussed. Some said it was the cutest baby they had ever seen and added nuanced terms to describe its distinctive complexion and looks. Terms such as coffee-colored, toffee-colored nice-tan with curly wooly-wavy type hair were used to highlight the baby's growing celebrity status.

A subdued discussion on the genealogy of the newborn was also taking place and increasing numbers of persons concluded the baby was of mixed race. Not surprisingly thoughts about its father's ethnic group and identity resulted in speculation since ethnic information on the mother and Provident family was known. Offers for adoption were pouring in from many families having obtained satisfactory information on the young mother. The anonymity of the father seemed to have allowed for easier resolve by those wishing to adopt the baby.

Dora had the inside track given her early caring of the baby and applied for adoption ahead of everyone else. Also Victor, the uncle and closest relative was domiciled at the Keswick home with all privileges of a family member, attested to a genial environment in the Keswick household.

A family-based claim was lodged by the Placide family led by Karen as the nearest of kin for custody of the baby. An undeniable argument was raised by Karen who pointed out the deceased mother at the time of the disaster was part of a commune living on family proprietary lands. The Hillside family of aunts and uncles, displayed general hostility towards all legality or referrals applied to determine the rights to custody and upbringing of the baby.

The opinion of Victor was crucial as the uncle of the newborn, brother of the deceased mother and only surviving member of the Provident clan. The authorities let it be known to all interested parties they were calling on him for guidance to resolve that matter hoping his decision would be highly respected and of primary benefit to the baby.

Victor was being coerced by his Hilltop family with humdrum comments like, "remember blood thicker than water," implying that he must favor his mother's and his blood relatives otherwise it would cause vexation and estrangement.

Meanwhile, the authorities advised Victor of yet another notable interest seeking to adopt the baby. It came from Mable and Diana. Victor was in total surprise and was further amazed to receive a summons-like request to visit the Baxter sisters at the suburban home of their brother. A chauffeured car provided, arrived at two p.m. hour ascertained as convenient by a reluctant Victor who was now unhappily placed in a pivotal role to resolve a three-way appeal for his support. His connectedness to the three parties, albeit for different reasons, was in each case significant and likely to incur displeasure and recriminations if dishonored. The situation seemed irreconcilable with no miracle or ruse to solve an adoption issue that had gained widespread interest and publicity across Au Tabor.

The Baxter sisters greeted Victor with Miss Mable leading the charge.

"First let me express my deepest sympathy on your loss. We were devastated when we heard of what had happened. So let us stand and say a prayer for those departed. Loving God, I pray you to welcome Victor's deceased family into Heaven with you. Forgive them their sins and reward them their goodness. Grant that we may be with them again in your peaceful presence and by means of our pious supplications; they may obtain the joy of Heaven, which they have earnestly desired. We ask this through Christ our Lord. Amen."

Without much pause, Diana and Victor resumed their seats and Miss Mable continued to preside over the meeting.

"A few days ago, your father sat right where you are to discuss your release from police custody. Of course, I readily agreed to give him all the help as I have always done. As you know, it was I who from early saw your promise and helped him set you off on your way. It is fair to say you have proven yourself a champion in every facet of endeavor, academic and sporting. In every encounter you have demonstrated courage, restraint and maturity as in when the police recklessly held you and in your reaction to young Blyth's insults. So this is why we heartily welcome you in remembrance of past relationships and above all to express sincere condolences on the tragic loss you have suffered."

It had never been easy to interject a Miss Mable monologue, especially when listing attributes and for which an indebted reaction and a grateful response were anticipated.

For Victor, it was a remarkable reenactment of his earliest days growing up in Baxter's Yard. On his arrival he was steered into the house and directed where to sit and following a review of his past and present circumstances, he was given an assessment of his progress with an implicit caution to continue conducting himself in an exemplary manner. He was not expected to return greetings with the same lofty wishes and flattery. To employ such privilege would imply self-importance and cheekiness. All that was necessary was a simple expression of thanks and a show of appreciation.

He thought of Lynette, recalling the exchanges in the bank's cafeteria and the conceit she may have derived from the surrounding family influence and accompanying prosperity to counter his attraction to Claire Beaufrand.

"Perhaps I should start where you left off," Victor attempted to give his perspective after the first clear pause. "Leaving Baxter's Yard was a significant departure and an important new beginning and I am indebted to the Keswick family for this new beginning and to the Baxter family for the first start. It is proving to be—."

"Please continue," Miss Mable interrupted, rising and excusing herself with obvious dislike for the meaning behind Victor's chat. "I am going to serve some snacks I prepared."

Immediately following Miss Mable's exit, Diana interjected aggressively in what appeared to be a prompt to begin the thorny role of a not so gentle persuasion, "Victor on the question of adoption we believe we will have your support. Our reason is more compelling than others who all have children and heirs that will be able to care for their parents and guardians. Even if either of us marries it is far too late for either of us to have children and see us through our later years."

"I was trying to explain earlier," Victor interrupted in an insistent tone that made Diana yield. "The difficult position is made worse because I am still trying to get over, and…and…." Victor choked and in an apparent out-of-control emotional outburst, got up abruptly and exclaimed, "Look, I don't care who they give the baby to, no one is talking about my whole family that is gone, gone, gone!" It was the first Victor behaved irrationally and his request to be driven back was granted without delay by the chauffeured car.

64

A decision on sponsors in the tradition of godfather, 'parwen' and godmother, 'nenen' had to wait the choice of would be guardians. There was a redeeming aspect in that irrespective of the diverse status of persons seeking to adopt the baby, everyone was unanimous the baby should be given the full name of the deceased mother, namely, Sophie Marie Bernadette Provident.

However it was the baptism of the week-old baby that gave impetus to the selection of a guardian and made the authorities feel vindicated. The selection was uncontested when Father Lambert made available the requisite parental information submitted in preparation for the baptism of his former parishioner's daughter:

Mother – Sophia Marie Bernadette Provident
Father – Vivian Gerald Keswick

The paternal name on the birth certificate surprised entire communities of Au Tabor. Many who had expressed contrary opinions about who should be granted adoptive rights were near unanimous in considering it a capricious act of the priest to submit the name of Vivian Keswick as father of the baby and moreover had broken the seal of confession and the Sacrament of Penance.

Many intensely religious persons, inclined to append to calamitous events as having mystical significance, did not accept the uninspiring logic of normal consequence. They were skeptical the arcane events leading up to a baby as sole survivor of the landslide, bore deeper meaning. The naming of a parent did not resolve for them why there were so many offers of adoption.

Father Lambert, a local Taborian priest was accused of misuse of his vows and powers by a varied group of citizens. Some people asserted that he was engaging in class mischief while those on Hillside opined that he did this in collaboration with the Keswick family so that they could have possession of the baby.

Father Lambert argued the name of a birth parent attached to a birth and baptismal certificate was a conditional requirement and not an issue of guilt or a matter for concealment. He was justified by the required affidavit from the father Vivian Keswick accepting paternity. This final stipulation sealed the decision to allow custody of Sophie Marie to go to the Keswick family.

After the baptismal ceremony, Dora thanked Father Lambert and in a conciliatory tone told him, "Father, this has not been as difficult as many are assuming, I felt an attachment to the baby the moment I saw it and my husband was fully in support of the adoption."

65

Dr. Keswick sought counseling for Victor in anticipation of his mental health being unable to withstand the horrors and vacuity from the loss of his immediate family.

Victor expressed to appointed counselors he had no substantive reason and desire to stick around, he did not want to be a living vestige of a family's calamitous ending. The alarm was sounded for a possible suicide attempt. Dr. Keswick took note and cautioned Victor to be cognizant he was the only Provident family link for his niece, baby Sophia, when she would later need ample testimony of her roots. He also reminded Victor of his interest in baby Sophia as she was also his granddaughter and through his association with Vivian, blood ties now exist between the Keswick and Provident families.

Victor remonstrated and requested him to make good on his promise to send him off to study overseas.

"Instead you should be telling me when I suppose to leave the island for study? All this blood business is because of your son, Vivian. Why am I the one responsible for blood ties? That is unfair. It is my family roots that died." Victor spoke defensively in short bursts. His breathing was heavy and intense and he had been having spells marked by emotional flare-ups since the tragic loss. His withdrawn and unfriendly responses were handled by the Keswicks with professional composure. Victor in some irrational moments judged his foster-parents as having placed obstacles, manufactured distractions, and locked the doors to hinder connectivity with his family.

At the request of Father Limos, Victor attended a meeting with other grieving mourners to set a date for a memorial mass for the lives lost as a result of the landslide.

The elected government of Au Tabor pressured by public sympathy also pronounced the day of the mass as a day of mourning and all flags were to be flown at half-mast.

The church overflowed with sympathizers with every seat taken. It was also an indication that the baby Sophia custody issue had been justly resolved and widely accepted. Among those in attendance were the Baxters, Beaufrands, Keswicks, the Pacscal and Alcide clan, the Innocent and Blyth families, Chalkie, Planche, Colom and Blackie, Nurse Grace and Hakim Mansur. Janie, Agnes, Katie, and Ma Reggie were in the forefront of a large Baxter's Yard contingent and perhaps the largest representation in numbers was from the Hillside District.

Father Limos in his sermon weighed in on a concern, which many in the congregation knew the individual for whose benefit it was being addressed.

"Many lost their loved ones without the opportunity to say goodbye, without a parting word, without a promise to meet again. This evoked a strong pledge to rejoin their family at the first opportunity; some are overanxious to fulfill that promise. This decision should be left to the Almighty God. It is his prerogative to make that decision because it was he who, in the first instance, gave us life. He will not receive us or join us with our loved ones if we decide on our own to end life. It was the sixth command handed down to Moses, 'Thou shall not kill' it did not refer to only others but also to thyself. Let us join the departed beforehand in spirit, let us choose a path of devotion to ensure the next meeting with them are on the terms mandated by his teaching."

Victor was visibly moved by the outpouring of support when the mass was over. He looked comforted surrounded by a sea of well-wishers hugging and pawing him affectionately. As Victor walked out of the churchyard he was flanked arm in arm on the right by Lynette Baxter and on his left by Claire Beaufrand

A few weeks after the day of mourning, Dr. Keswick thought Victor sufficiently stable after his ordeal and concluded arrangements for him to begin studies beginning with the January Hilary term.

EPILOGUE

The decade following was recorded on a generational clock. Changes in musical, sexual, and scientific approaches negated past methods and customs. Those no longer fashionable were relegated as traditions to be later crafted and portrayed in various art forms for the enrichment of local heritage.

The political timepiece recorded two election cycles; the governing party lost its mandate after ten years in office. There was a mild tropical storm in year two flooding the town and washing away the bridge crossing the Angier River. A strike on a sugar estate in year two turned violent and order had to be restored by police in riot gear. In year three, a Royal Princess Alice stepped onto our shores for a one-day visit and in the ninth year the royal yacht berthed at the docks as consort to a group of visiting dignitaries.

Such were the milestones in the monthly letters of correspondence, which had their first reading a few steps from the post box.

Particularly in the latter half of the study year, absorption of personals in the letter had to await a return to the chilly confines of a rented room where all necessary chores of cooking, eating, studying and sleeping took place. In the letters from home obituaries, illnesses, tragic events and local hardships were appearing more frequently.

Girlfriends had difficulty maintaining a fervent love, wavering in fidelity. This distracted Martin and adversely affected his studies.

Au Tabor recipients of return mail experienced a glow of warmth in their hearts in spite of opening sentences relating woeful tales of cold winter days and loneliness. A yearning for local dishes, friends, family and surrounds yielded discomforting expression.

Tropical Island anchored in the wake of unrelenting seas spawned by oceans from afar, vacillates as each new breaking wave crashes against a charred land, once home to a downtrodden crew now buried under.

www.ingramcontent.com/pod-product-compliance
Lightning Source LLC
Chambersburg PA
CBHW020639260626
47157CB00008B/2826